HER SWORN ENEMY
MEN OF THE ZODIAC

THERESA MEYERS

Entangled Publishing, LLC
2614 South Timberline Road
Suite 109
Fort Collins, CO 80525
Visit our website at www.entangledpublishing.com.

Indulgence is an imprint of Entangled Publishing, LLC.

Edited by Alethea Spiridon Hopson
Cover design by Heather Howland
Cover art from iStock and Shutterstock

Manufactured in the United States of America

First Edition December 2015

*For those that love the sea, may the waves ever be entrancing
and the wind bring you home. And for all the Pisces who
have graced my life, Jerry Meyers, Chloe Meyers, Ron Sauro,
Bruce Homstad, Keath Ronk, and Matt Baehr, thank you
for letting me see just how amazing this sign can be. For Jim
Somerville for some of my favorite nonsensical words in
everyday conversation like wiggitywhack. Last, but never
least, in memory of James (Jim) Williams, may you rest in
peace and know how many lives you touched at Sedgwick
Junior High. You were an inspiration.*

Chapter One

"Change is coming, *cher*. You'd know this if you read your horoscope."

Belladonna Dupré mumbled something unintelligible to her aunt in response and stared harder at the numbers in front of her, willing them to change, anything to make their situation better.

"Bella?"

She loved her aunt, adored her really, but woo-woo wasn't going to fix the problems they had. Bella glanced up. "No, because some half-baked journalist predicting events by astrological signs isn't going to make any difference in solving our debt problem."

"You know, if you keep spreading such negativity in here, I'm going to have to use a smudge stick around the shop to clear it. Not to mention you're going to have serious frown lines in the middle of your forehead by the time you're my age."

Bella forced her features to relax and modulated her tone. Getting angry at her aunt wasn't a solution. "Well, if the universe would stop being such a serious nudge, maybe I'd be more positive. Despite what my horoscope, the cards, or any other divination might say, the facts say we're screwed."

Her aunt finished stocking the tourist mugs emblazoned with little voodoo dolls and *fleurs-de-lis* on the shelf then folded down the flaps on the cardboard box and glanced at her. "Just how bad is it?"

The fan overhead beat in slow, lazy circles, doing little more than stirring a current in the stifling humid air that smelled of muddy river off the Mississippi, wet paving bricks from the French Quarter, and the too pungent odor of antiseptic wipes in the tattoo portion of the shop. They'd economized to the point where they barely ran the air conditioning at Inkspell, and never at home.

Bella's job as an antiquities appraiser, preservationist, and restoration expert at Fontanel & Company, combined with her aunt's gift shop slash tattoo parlor, barely kept them afloat. Once upon a time the Dupré family had been one of the wealthiest Cajun families in New Orleans. How far they'd fallen. A string of unfortunate incidents, a few bad investments, and the kick of a national financial crisis and they'd been reduced down to basics. But, if Bella had anything to say about it, that was about to change.

"What do you want to hear first, the good news or the bad news?" she snapped as she wadded up the bill in disgust and threw it on the long black countertop. It hit the cash register, then dropped to the scarred plank floor. Crumpled dreams and crushing debt.

Her aunt sighed. "Well, considering the last time you had bad news it was that my mother passed away, I think I'd rather hear the good news first." Minunette, who was only fifteen years older than her niece, set the box down next to the scrunched up ball of paper.

"The good news is we get to keep the shop doors open."

For a few more months at least. But that bad news could wait.

Min smiled. It was a warm smile, the kind that went to her pale green eyes, that comforted Bella and reminded her so much of the mother and grandmother that had raised her. But Min was anything but a typical Dupré woman who lived and died in the heart of New Orleans. Her riot of dark curls was piled up high on her head in a messy bun held in place with a pen, and her bare shoulder in her black heavy metal band tank top had a tattoo of a wheel of the zodiac. She was the family rebel who'd used her artistic skills with tattoos to travel the world. "That is good news. I wasn't sure we would, considering how upset you seemed by Mr. Ruesard's letter about the loan."

"That's only because you haven't heard the bad news."

Min's smile faded, and worry clouded her eyes. "What?"

"Along with agreeing to the extension, he's increasing the interest rate—again." Their gazes locked. They were barely squeaking by as it was. "*Mon dieu*, why doesn't he just take the skin off our backs, since he's already taken the shirts!"

Aunt Min's eyes turned hard, and she pointed a stern index finger in Bella's direction. "That's no way to talk about Mr. Ruesard. He's been very patient in allowing us to pay back the loan in installments for far longer than he should have."

"Yes, but if Harry would just let me pull up the cargo of the *Rapid*, we would've paid this off by now."

Min shook her head, grabbed a dust cloth, and began wiping down the counter. "Don't blame your boss because we can't escape fate."

"Fate? Is that what you call that bastard investment company that wiped out what little we had left in our accounts after the recession with their bad decisions?" Paying for her two degrees in an effort to learn all she could to find the wreck, and repaying the bank loan were the biggest chunks of their debt. If things didn't improve soon, she would find a third job beyond Fontanel & Company and Inkspell to fix this mess. One way or another, she refused to let down what little family she had left.

"That's not the point. Between that unfortunate situation, and what you've spent on your education searching for that wreck on the bottom of the ocean that you seem to believe could save us, there's nothing left. It's not Ruesard's fault."

Her aunt was absolutely right. That didn't make the situation any more palatable. It only made Bella feel guilty as hell that she'd sucked up their resources to get the education she needed. Between that expense, and being screwed by the first man she'd trusted enough to hand over what little money they had for investment, and the crooked investment company he'd recommended, they were now screwed.

Bella was angry. With herself for falling for Phillip McCormack, who'd turned out to be a smooth-talking con man, and for entrusting the wrong people to manage their money. No, it wasn't the *bank's* fault. It was *her* fault.

She had to make this right. Had. To.

Salvaging the *Rapid* had always been a romantic fantasy. She'd grown up hearing the story of her ancestor captain on board who'd acted as a privateer, amassing a fortune—a large portion of it aboard the *Rapid* when it went down. There was even the thrilling possibility that they'd been transporting a crystal ball of "great value." A great value in 1812 could mean a mega fortune today. Everything she'd done, everything she'd studied, everywhere Bella had worked, was because she hoped one day to salvage the *Rapid*. It was a dream, an exciting, fun thing to look forward to.

But the romantic "one day" fantasy had now turned into a grim reality, with a loudly ticking clock. If she had a hope in hell of saving their house, and Min's business, Bella had to have a quick infusion of cash. Real money to pay off their crushing debt.

"True," she said, her chest aching with the pressure building up. Hope. "But, Min, that's our birthright. You know how wealthy we'd be if I could only get to it?"

Min held up her hand. "Stop. That's enough. We've made it through worse. Dream all you like, but you need to live in the here and now. There may not be anything left to salvage. For all we know, in the past two hundred years someone else got to the *Rapid,* and it was looted long ago. It's a family story. We owe Mr. Ruesard the money, and getting angry with him isn't going to solve anything." Her tone had an undercurrent of finality Bella knew better than to challenge.

Yeah, well, it may not solve anything, but being angry at Ruesard instead of herself made Bella feel better. Sometimes it felt as if the entire universe were conspiring against her. The treasure onboard the *Rapid* was out there. She knew it. Not in her heart of hearts like some touchy-feely thing, but actually *knew* where it was with scientific facts. She'd managed to pinpoint the location after years of painstaking research, and it was just sitting out there, calling to her, waiting for her to claim it. It would take money to get at it. Money they didn't have. The catch-22 was it took money to make money.

Bella clenched her hands on the edges of the counter. Too bad she couldn't glare at the bill on the floor and make it burst into flame. The annoying weasel of a bank manager was closer to a loan shark in her opinion. He was charging them usury interest rates and had already laid claim to the shop's tattoo equipment as collateral on the loan. What the hell else did they have? Everything, even their family home for seven generations, was mortgaged to the hilt.

There were three things Bella knew for sure: one, money might not make the world go round, but it sure as hell never hurt; two, the Dupré women had a thing for bad boys that never worked out to their advantage; and three, if there was such a thing as fate, which she didn't believe, she was a total, nasty bitch.

It was the only explanation for why time and again every opportunity for the Dupré family to regain the position and respect they'd once enjoyed had been wrecked in the shoals of misfortune. Either that, or just like her *grand-mère* had said, they were cursed, and Bella didn't believe in that, either. For once, she'd like the stars to align and the universe to bring some unexpected good into her life.

Snatching up her purse, she threw the thin leather strap over her shoulder and swung around the counter. "I'm going to be late for work if I don't get moving."

"Invite positive things into your life, and try to have a good day," Aunt Min said and waved as she picked up the boxes and carried them to the back room. The brightly colored bead curtain covering the doorway clicked as she passed through then swayed back into place.

Positive. Fine, she would be more positive. Perhaps Aunt Min was right, and change, hopefully for the better, was coming. The front door, propped open to let in some more air, seemed like an escape hatch. Bella marched toward it, staring at the phone in her hand, and slammed straight into a hard wall of muscle.

For a moment the impact took her breath away, knocking her off her feet. She landed on her butt with a painful jolt. Her phone skittered across the wooden floor worn smooth by thousands of footsteps over the years. Her already foul mood and the knowledge that she'd been at fault, even though she was certain she'd taken the worst of the incident, sent a wave of hot embarrassment flooding into her system.

"Are you all right?" The male voice was smooth and deep.

She glanced up at the human wall that had blocked the door and found her breathing compromised again, this time because she realized the man she'd collided with was drop-dead gorgeous.

"I didn't see you." The second the words left her mouth she realized how utterly stupid they sounded. How could you *not* see him? Well over six feet tall and big enough to fill the doorway, he wasn't someone you could easily miss. Tack on a pair of stunning blue eyes, like the gulf on a hot summer's day, paired with thick, dark brows, rugged features, and surfer blond hair and he was sex on the beach wrapped in a tight, dark blue T-shirt and low-slung khaki shorts.

He offered her a hand, easily two sizes bigger than her own, to help her up from the floor. Even though she didn't want to take it, ignoring the help would be stupid, and she'd already done enough to make herself look like a fool for one morning.

The moment she slid her hand into his, an arc of awareness zipped along her nerve endings. Every cell took notice. With effortless ease he pulled her up.

"Have we met before?" Again her mouth betrayed her. Should have kept that to herself.

An easy, cocky half grin lifted the edge of an all-too-kissable mouth as he picked up her phone and offered it to her. "No, but I wouldn't mind an introduction."

Bella's gaze caught the time on the display of her phone. Even upside down, she could tell she was late. She yanked her hand out of his grasp, grabbed her phone, and flashed him an apologetic smile. "Sorry. Got to go. I'm late."

For a moment William Tucker McCormack considered standing where he was so she couldn't get out. He really did want an introduction. She had killer curves, stunning pale green eyes, long dark hair, and a deceptively sweet, almost pixie-like face that obviously hid a spicy side that intrigued him. But she was flustered enough, so he let her past him, then kicked himself for not even getting her name, let alone her number. In her wake, he caught hints of lemonade and sugar cookies in the air.

If he was going to make the most of this trip to New Orleans, he ought to be taking up the opportunities when he came across them, especially since he'd have no time for fun once he and his recovery team got down to business in a week or two. He'd only come to Inkspell because his buddy Russ recommended Min Dupré as a one-of-a-kind tattoo artist. Tuck had always wanted a tattoo. Until now, he'd refrained for various reasons. Mostly because a tattoo seemed, well, permanent, and he didn't do permanent. But since he was on potentially the biggest gig of his independent career, it seemed like the perfect way to both celebrate the moment and at the same time give his stuffy, obscenely wealthy, autocratic family a big middle finger in style. A tat would make his father roll over in his grave. Body art was for lowlifes according to the old man. It simply wasn't done, especially not by a McCormack.

The thought made Tuck smile as he walked inside. It was several degrees cooler in the shade of the shop, and the fan overhead help stir up a breeze that smelled of lavender and dried herbs. He scanned the various pictures on the wall. Damn. They were all spectacular. True to his buddy's word, the lady was an outstanding artist. Just the shading and lines alone made each tattoo come alive.

The colorful bead curtain covering the doorway to the back of the shop shifted, the beads clicking together as a woman with a curtain of dark wavy hair and familiar pale green eyes moved toward the counter. She was pretty, and Tuck bet in her younger years she'd been a bit on the wild side. While her mouth wasn't as lush and her hair was darker, she looked similar to the mystery woman who'd run into him. Her sleeveless tank top revealed a curvy body and a tattoo of the wheel of the zodiac on her right shoulder.

She smiled. "Can I help you?"

"Hi, I'm looking for Min Dupré."

"Well, *cher*, you found me." She slid an assessing gaze over him, as if to see if he measured up, and he noticed the female appreciation in her eyes. "How'd you hear of me?"

"A friend said your tattoos are lucky. And"—he gestured to the wall displaying her skill—"looking at these, I'd say they're beautiful as well."

"What kind of design were you thinking of?"

He shrugged. "Does it matter?"

The woman's gaze locked with his. The glint in the sea-green depth of her eyes told him it did, very much.

"A tattoo is a personal mark. It can define you."

He glanced back again at the images on the wall behind her, looking at the designs and discarding them just as quickly, now that it came to picking something personal to him. Only one image captured his attention. It was close, but not right.

"What about that, only different?" He pointed to the *S* like swirl of black and white in a circle with opposing dots of color forming a yin yang symbol.

"The taijitu? Certainly. How would you like it to be different?" To him, her tone sounded as if she were testing him, waiting to see if he came up with a satisfactory answer that would somehow give her insight into him.

Tuck stared at the image until it started to swim in his vision. "Fish. I want two koi fish, one black, one white, on my shoulder."

"You're a Pisces." It wasn't a question. When he nodded, she said briskly, "A good choice, hopefully one that brings you balance and harmony."

Tuck needed neither balance nor harmony, but he could do with a bit of luck. If the salvage op was anything like it was suggested to be, he'd finally break free from the shadow of his family and prove to his moocher half siblings and cousins that just because you came from money didn't mean you couldn't get off your freeloading ass, go out, and earn it yourself.

There was only one other thing he wanted to achieve after making a name for himself—revenge. He wanted to stick it to his older half brother, Phillip, who'd stripped both him and his mother of everything when James McCormack had passed away, leaving them destitute and forced to take only what they could carry when they moved into a shelter.

When he was done with Phillip, he would know what loss felt like. Tucker would buy out the McCormack Company in a hostile takeover from under his half brother, then dismantle it. He'd prove, bastard son or not, he was more than just a McCormack. He was his own man, and he'd leave his own mark on the world.

He watched intently as Min Dupré began to sketch his tattoo on a translucent sheet of transfer paper, the tip of her pencil moving rapidly. Rather than make it a perfect outline of a circle, she let the fins of each fish flow freely at the outer edges, giving it the illusion of the yin yang symbol, but a freedom of movement that made it seem natural and flowing, like water. Two fish. Exact opposites but totally united. Perfect.

She lifted her pencil and looked him in the eye. "Is this what you had in mind?"

In a way it was kind of freakish how she'd drawn what he saw in his mind so precisely down to the scales on the fish. "Yeah. That's great!"

"If you go ahead and have a seat over there, you can make yourself comfortable while you fill out these," she said, indicating a reclining chair in the corner with a small workstation and a large mirror on the wall beside it as she handed him some paperwork. "I'll be back in a few minutes to get started."

Tuck took his time getting to the chair and looked at the

other curious items on display in the shop. No use rushing things. It seemed like Inkspell was part tattoo parlor, part occult shop—nothing that seemed out of the ordinary in the French Quarter. One wall sported nothing but shelf after shelf of large glass jars, all neatly labeled, containing various dried herbs, seeds, and nuts. A few even had bones. There were crystals and tarot cards, mugs, and books. He settled into the chair and finished filling out the permission and health form just before the tattoo artist returned.

She flipped through his papers, laid them aside on the workstation, and slipped on a pair of thin latex gloves. She took a bottle of dark green soap from the counter, wet down his skin, and cleaned the area to be tattooed, then transferred the design to his shoulder.

"So what brings you to New Orleans, business or pleasure?"

He gave her a wicked smile. "I'm hoping a bit of both. I'm starting a new job in the next week."

"What kind of work do you do?"

"Salvage and recovery."

"Buildings?"

"Wrecks."

She lifted one dark brow. "So you're a treasure hunter?"

"It's not hunting if you already know where to find it."

"Interesting line of work." She turned her attention back to his tattoo.

As she worked he focused on something beyond the buzzing sound and sharp sting of the needle working its magic to create a masterpiece. Fortunately, he had the perfect thing to distract him. "I bumped into a young lady who looks a lot like you when I came into the shop. Are you two related?"

Min's gaze never left the work she was doing on his shoulder. "That's my niece, Belladonna."

Score one for his side. He had her name.

"Is she an artist like you?"

The corner of Min's mouth twitched. "No, Bella's far more practical and pragmatic. She's not one to flit where the wind takes her."

So, the kind who wanted to settle down. Strike one. Not good. "She works here with you?"

For a moment the needle lifted from his skin, and Min wiped the blood away from her work, making eye contact in the mirror. "Only to help out here and there. Why, are you interested?"

He gave her a genuine smile. "Do you seriously know a man who isn't? She's gorgeous."

Min chuckled. "Well, at least you know how to speak the truth. Our Bella is easy on the eyes, but don't let that fool you. That girl's got a temper."

What the hell, might as well go for a home run. "Husband? Boyfriend? Significant other?"

Min's eyes twinkled. "Not yet."

Chapter Two

"You wanted a professional dive and recovery team, and I've got you one that our investors approved. You'll have three months to find and recover the *Rapid*. After that I'm pulling the plug. We're cutting it close to hurricane season as it is," her boss, Harold Palmer, told Bella as she sat in his office.

Bella stared at him. "That's fantastic! Who's the investor?"

"They've requested anonymity, and I'm respecting that request."

Bella digested that for a moment. This was similar to Phillip's assurance that she should take his recommendation of the investment company on blind faith. "Look, it's not that I'm ungrateful, but why won't you tell me who's funding our project?" *And why do I feel like there's a catch?*

Harold shook his head and chuckled. "I understand your need to have all the i's dotted and the t's crossed, but in this case you'll have to take it or leave it. The investor isn't budging on this point. They've asked to remain anonymous as a condition of providing the remaining funds for the project."

She wasn't going to look a gift horse in the mouth. "What's the catch?" Because fate ensured there was always a catch.

"I get fifty percent of the find."

She narrowed her eyes. Not unexpected, but if it wasn't for her, Harold wouldn't even have known the wreck existed. "Are *you* the investor?"

"If I was, it wouldn't be anonymous, but no. I'm not."

"How much do they want?"

"Fifty percent."

More than fair when they were funding the operation. Bella's lips twitched. "So *you* get fifty percent, and *they* get fifty percent, and that leaves zero percent for me. Not much of incentive for me, is it? Ten percent for your trouble."

Ten percent of nothing was nothing. Ten percent of what she hoped, suspected, and prayed was beneath the ocean would be, literally, a drop in the bucket financially.

Harold's chair creaked as he leaned back, a glint in his eye. "Twenty."

"Fifteen, and that's only because you found a financial backer for the project, and if I find my ancestor's crystal ball, I get to keep it. Without a percentage."

Harold nodded and smiled. "Remember, doc, you gotta ask. Never know what you can get until you ask for it. You find this wreck, and fifteen percent will be more than enough for me to retire."

Bella snorted. "As if you could. You're a damn workaholic, Harold, and you know it."

Harold winked at her. "True, but you can't stop a man from dreaming."

"So who's this salvage operator you've hired?"

The air stirred in the office, and she sensed a distinctly male presence behind them.

"Tucker McCormack at your service," said a man's smooth voice from the doorway. "I'm your dive salvage expert."

Bella turned and stared at the tanned man whose massive shoulders filled the doorway. The same wall of man had knocked her on her ass at her aunt's shop just a week before.

"Pleasure to see you again," he said simply, mouth turning up at the edges with humor.

When she'd first seen him in the shop, she thought her mind had been playing tricks on her. Not every big, gorgeous guy reminded her of Phillip. But that angular jaw, those clear blue eyes under dark intense brows, and most of all, that arrogant, smug smile made her do a double take.

He looked similar to Phillip McCormack, too similar for her comfort. Oh, he was far less slick and polished and far more fit and tan, but there was no way in hell she would ever trust a McCormack again. Not after Phillip had basically gambled away what little she and *grand-mère* had left of their inheritance on bad investments, leaving them practically out on the street until *grand-mère* had passed away and her aunt had come back to New Orleans recently to open Inkspell.

"Are you related to Phillip McCormack?" Holding back her thoughts was not her strong suit. In fact, frequently she had no filter between her thoughts and what popped out of her mouth.

He shrugged. "Unfortunately, and in a roundabout way. Don't get to pick your family, you know." Bella folded her arms into a protective shield over her chest. Maybe her instincts weren't that far off. Maybe he was a cousin. She'd been far too attracted to him at the shop for a mere stranger, even though technically that's exactly what he was.

She saw her rosy future dissipating right before her eyes. "I'm sorry, I can't work with you."

McCormack's eyes narrowed. "What?"

"You're a McCormack."

"And what does that have to do with me?"

"Your family thinks they can take whatever they want,

without consequences and without giving a damn who else is involved. Isn't 'Take everything. Give nothing back.' your family motto? I don't trust you." She couldn't be plainer than that.

He put up his hands, as if pushing back hard on the words she flung at him. "Whoa. Look, I don't know where you got the idea that my relatives have anything to do with how I behave, but I can assure you, I'm nothing like them. Never have been." The intensity in his eyes and the fine tick in his jaw revealed their association was tense.

Out of the corner of her eye she spied Harold pouring himself a drink and sitting back to watch the fireworks. That was fine with her. She didn't need Harold or any other man to save her. As far as she was concerned, she planned on breaking the losing streak that had plagued the women in her family, and that started by taking care of things for herself.

"How are you related to Phillip?"

Storm clouds shot with lightning gathered in his eyes. "Normally I don't answer personal questions like that in business meetings."

"Indulge me."

The sudden glint in his eye said he'd like to…in a very hands-on fashion.

Oh girl, do not tempt him. Bella was too amped up to listen to the voice of reason in her head.

"Since this seems to be a sticking point for you, he's my older half brother. We share a sperm donor and not much else."

Liar. Phillip had two sisters. No brothers. She'd had dinner with all of them, once upon a time when she'd had the foolish belief that Phillip wanted to marry her and that she wasn't just his college booty call.

"Funny, he never mentioned having a brother."

"Yeah. He wouldn't. My mom's the mistress, so technically,

in his world, I don't exist." The hard edge to his tone indicated she'd treaded on a tender subject.

Way to step in it, girl. Everyone had their share of dark family secrets. Bella shifted uncomfortably in her chair. "Hardly your fault."

Tuck shrugged and moved easily across the room settling his big frame in a chair right beside her. Bella could feel the palpable male energy rolling off him like a heat wave. "No big deal. Can't miss what you never had, right?"

She wished that were true, but on so many levels, it wasn't. She felt bound to her family and her home and knew she'd never want or need the freedom to go anywhere and try anything that her aunt seemed to achieve so flawlessly. Home was her sanctuary.

She wanted the kind of man who would sink down roots and grow old with her, something permanent like the big, mossy oaks that lasted centuries on the plantations where they'd first been planted. God knew she'd never come across a dependable male yet, and that included her own father. But more than either of those things she never had, Bella missed the awe and respect wealth bought in a society where there were still prejudices going back generations. Here the words Creole and Cajun weren't just tourist terms, but deeper degrees of freedom and color, power and wealth, and a family's place in society.

"I thought there were only three kids in Phillip's family."

"Yeah. His side. Never met any of them. But apparently he gets to be Prince Phillip at home, since he's the *only* boy." There was enough rancor in the way he said "only" that Bella could tell it bothered him.

"Shall we get back on point?" he said in a tone that indicated he had no intention of continuing to discuss his family.

Bella hesitated. "I need to know one more thing before I

can decide if I'll work with you."

"What?"

"*Why* do you want to work on this project?"

Intense blue eyes locked with hers. Bella sucked in a breath at the spark of awareness that shot all the way to her toes and made her girly parts sit up and take notice.

Tucker McCormack was not a man to be manipulated, which meant she was going to have her work cut out for her. So she did what any sane woman would do when she wanted something and had obviously just pissed off the person who could make her dream a reality. She appealed to his ego. "What I mean is, well, if you are a McCormack, you obviously have more money than you possibly need. So, what's the draw for you in this? It's pocket change where you come from." If it was possible, he looked even more pissed off by her comment. Great.

"That's an interesting assumption to make when you don't know the first thing about me." His voice was cool, and his eyes telegraphed his annoyance. "It isn't about the money. Never has been."

Easy to say if one had plenty of it, Bella thought bitterly, but kept her mouth shut.

He splayed his fingers through his hair, making the golden tips stand on end. "Haven't you ever had a dream? Something you wanted so bad you'd do anything to get it?"

A bubble of excitement welled up inside her chest, and she nodded. Of course she had. Why else take this fool's risk on the *Rapid*?

"Sure." Bringing up the *Rapid* had been her dream as long as she could remember, the one that had caused the rift between her and Phillip. When he'd told her it was him or the *Rapid*, she'd chosen the *Rapid*. That had been a blow his ego couldn't take, so he'd dumped her.

"You okay?" The rough edge of his voice shook her out of her thoughts.

"Yes. Dream. Please continue."

He looked at her a moment, his eyes drilling into her, sampling her soul. He must have found something he was looking for, because he continued. "Well, my dream is to make a name for myself, a name that has nothing to do with the *McCormack* name. I want a legacy. I want my time on Earth to mean something."

Bella felt any connection beyond attraction to him was lost again. Just because Tucker was at odds with his family, and bore them a great deal of resentment, apparently, didn't mean he wasn't part of it, even if that part was only financial. If his mother had been the father's mistress, he must've provided well for her and his son.

This guy wasn't financially destitute. She couldn't even conceive of the kind of power and influence his family held in their deep pockets, and yet he was acting like it was the bane of his existence. Hell, she was happy to make sure their mortgages got paid so they weren't out on the streets. He might claim to have been down and out once upon a time, but he came from wealth and the rarified air of it still clung to him.

"And how is this project going to help you?"

"You can keep half of whatever your salvage operator's cut of the find would normally be." He paused a beat.

Bella had to admit that was a good deal, hell, an amazing deal, far better than she'd hoped. "What's the catch?"

"I want full credit for the find."

Whoa. And there was the deal breaker.

Suddenly, she didn't give a damn if he'd been approved by the project's secret financial backer or not. Just like Phillip, he wanted to deny her what belonged to her by birthright. Bella shot up out of her chair. "You what?"

"Didn't I say it plainly enough?"

Searing heat blazed through her, like a reflux of strong hot sauce, welling up in her throat and making her flush. "Do *not* patronize me. I heard you fine. I simply can't believe what you said, because it was completely asinine."

He shrugged. "What? I'm not asking for full payment for the project. I think that getting full credit in exchange is fair."

The hell it was. She took a step closer to him, getting in his personal space.

"Do you have any idea how long it took me to track this ship down? How much family history I had to dig through, and shipping logs, manifests. Do you have any clue how hard I worked to get my damned degrees in the first place to get this job so I could *find* the *Rapid*?"

He blinked a couple of times. "Did I do something to piss you off?"

"Yeah, you want to take credit for my life's work and my family legacy." She stared him down, crossing her arms. "Forget it. I'll find another salvage operator."

He crossed his arms. "The financial backer on the project wants me. Without me, it's a non-starter."

"Fine. Then I'll find another backer."

With that, she spun on her heel, fists swinging by her sides as she marched out of Harold's office.

Tuck watched her perfect ass sashay out the door. Her aunt hadn't been wrong. Belladonna Dupré had a hair trigger when it came to her anger issues. Then again, if someone had come to him and asked for credit for his life's work, he'd be offended, too. Problem was, he'd never committed long enough to any one thing to become known for more than his birthright as the illegitimate son of James McCormack, multi-billionaire.

The second problem was that he could see why Phillip had been taken with her. And if he truly intended to get back at

Phillip, he had to shove away any notion that this was for the long term. He was here to get what he needed to undercut Phillip and overtake the family holdings. In. Out. Done. No attachments. No strings. Nothing to tie him down and ruin his life.

He blinked for a moment, trying to clear the image of Bella walking out the door and turned back to Harold. "Is she always like that?"

Harold shook his head and smiled. "No, son. You seem to really bring it out in her. I've only seen Doc Dupré go off like that once before." He leaned back in his chair giving Tucker an assessing look. "You still sure you want to be the pocketbook *and* muscle behind this expedition?"

"Did you tell her I was underwriting the project?"

"Did it look like it? Doc may have a temper, but she's as smart as a whip. She wouldn't intentionally piss off an investor in a recovery and research project she's been bugging me about for the last five years." Clearly, Harold both respected the woman and knew her well.

"So she wants it badly."

"Worse than she wants anything else."

That was good to know. Wanting things or people was a weakness. Might give him an edge.

"You're real quiet. Having second thoughts?" Harold asked.

Tuck smiled. "If anything, I'm more intrigued. Who do I write the check out to?"

By the time she reached the cataloging rooms on the ground floor, Bella had nearly gotten control of her heartbeat again. Unfortunately, she hadn't done as well with her anger. The only thing that tempered it was realizing how unprofessional she'd been.

Without an experienced dive and recovery crew, she could kiss good-bye any chance of bringing the treasures from the *Rapid* up to the surface. She had the information, education, and historical knowledge to know where the wreck was, what condition it might be in, how to find it, and what it might be worth, but her diving experience was limited to snorkeling and swimming pools. She'd been looking for a financial backer for years. They weren't easy to find.

Bella bit her lip and sagged against a concrete and brick wall, her head tipping back to rest against the cool, hard surface. Harold would demand she apologize. But for what? For saying the truth? McCormack basically wanted to claim everything she'd scrimped and scraped for, every tear she'd shed in the last ten years, every ounce of blood and sweat she'd put into getting her dual Ph.D. degrees in maritime archeology and history in the first place, all so he could show up his daddy, or his big brother, or both. She huffed out a frustrated breath.

Not that she had any right as the pot to call the kettle black. She had a heaping helping of her own daddy issues on her plate. But what if in that morass of stupid issues, they could find common ground? What if she could convince McCormack to share the credit for the find, rather than take it all for himself? Could she live with that?

No.

Maybe.

It all depended on what it would take to convince him.

She went into the lab, picked up the desk phone, and called Harold's office. Using her cell phone in the middle of the concrete building didn't work worth beans.

Harold's secretary Margret answered. "Mr. Palmer's office."

Bella gave thanks to God for small favors. "Margret, this is Bella. Is Harold still talking with that dive-recovery consultant?"

"Hang on a second." The line went static as Bella's pulse bumped up the pace with worry.

"Yeah, he's still here, but it looks like they're finishing up. Did you want Harold to call you back when he's done?"

"No. Actually, can you keep the consultant there for a few minutes until I can get back upstairs?"

"Sure, honey."

Bella hung up the phone, flipped her hair upside down, and fluffed it a bit, then grabbed a quick swipe of lipstick from her bag, pinched her cheeks, and put on a spritz of her favorite lemon verbena body mist. Feeling marginally better, she took a deep breath, dug deep for her best southern manners, and headed back up stairs.

"I told you Dr. Dupré is the best historical artifacts expert we have." Harold's voice drifted out of his office before Bella turned the corner.

"Yes, but do you think she can handle a project of this scope if she's this emotionally unstable?"

"Oh, the doc ain't unstable. Just stubborn as hell," Harold replied.

Shit. Yes, she'd gone and made quite an impression with McCormack. *Great. Just great.*

She pasted a smile she didn't feel onto her lips, lifted her chin, and pulled back her shoulders, as poised as any genteel southern girl on the beauty pageant runway, and walked up to Harold's door, then rapped on the doorframe.

The conversation abruptly stopped, and they both stared at her. "I've come to offer an apology for my rude behavior earlier."

"I appreciate that," McCormack said. "But it doesn't give me much hope we can work together."

"Now don't be too hard on her, Mr. McCormack. She's a brilliant scientist and historian. I tell you, you won't find better in the Crescent City."

"So you've said. Repeatedly."

Bella took a step into the office. "I don't blame you for having reservations, but try and understand how passionate I am about this project. It's not just another find to me. It's my family legacy."

"I understand, but as I said, I'm not in it for the money. I want the recognition."

Exactly what she wanted. Well—she wanted the money *and* recognition. Bella chewed thoughtfully on her bottom lip. Would she be willing to share the credit for her find if it made the difference between finding another backer for the dive and potentially never getting to see the treasures aboard the *Rapid*, or getting to do this here and now before Ruesard kicked them out of their home and took Aunt Min's business? *Yes.* She could do that.

"What if we were to share the credit? Would that suffice?"

He raised an imperious dark brow. "Fine. If we share the credit for the find, then I want twenty-five percent."

Despite her best intentions, she frowned. "I thought you weren't in it for the money."

"I'm not, but neither am I naive. If I'm not going to get the benefit of full credit for the find, I might as well make up for it in another way. That's fair, isn't it?"

"I think that's more than fair," Harry interjected. Bella forced herself to shove the simmering, angry heat in her belly down low. *Think of the Rapid. Think of the treasure. Do what you have to do to make this happen, girl.*

She inhaled deeply and held her breath for a moment. "Obviously in this circumstance, it doesn't matter what I think or don't think. We need to rely on the facts."

"And those are?"

"I know where the ship is and what we need to do to preserve, authenticate, catalog, and market anything we find properly, but I can't bring it to the surface without you and your crew."

McCormack gave one curt nod of acknowledgement.

"And you won't do it without sharing the credit for the find and a percentage."

He nodded again.

"Twenty percent," she said, crossing her arms.

"I believe I said twenty-five."

"You did. And you also want me to share credit for the find, which makes it twenty percent."

McCormack glanced at Harold. "You said she was smart. You didn't tell me she was a barracuda in negotiations."

Harold gave a satisfied grin. "You won't find better, I guarantee it."

The way Harold said it with his deep southern drawl, guarantee sounded more like gay-ron-tee, but Tuck didn't care. Five percent? He wasn't about to lose out on this opportunity over five percent. Let her think she won. He was here on a mission of his own that had nothing to do with her. From his family and rocky life, he'd learned that people who were given things didn't appreciate them nearly as much as those who had to work for those same things. So he'd take his twenty percent and make her believe she'd worked for the concession.

"Fine, twenty percent and joint credit on the find." He held out his hand.

Her hand slowly rose to meet his. Like at Inkspell, just the slide of her bare skin against his, even in something so basic as a handshake, gave him an instant rush that both surprised and unsettled him. He'd been attracted to a lot of women before, but this was different, as if sparks pulsed through her in a current of energy and he plugged into it just by touching her.

"Okay, you've got yourself a deal, Mr. McCormack."

"Please, call me Tuck. My father was Mr. McCormack."

"And your older brother?"

"Dickhead, but he doesn't prefer it."

Her eyes sparkled. There was more to Belladonna Dupré than met the eye, although what met the eye was damn tempting to start with. Her movements were graceful and flowing, like a mermaid in the water, which only accentuated the flair of her hips and her inviting curves. Her pale green eyes reminded him of sea glass. His gaze dropped to the very full lips he bet were softer than the satin smooth skin on her hand. And she smelled so good he wanted to see if her skin really did taste like sugar cookies and lemonade. He resisted the instant urge to kiss her and reluctantly let her hand slide from his.

Tucker pulled his libido in on a short leash. Damn. It would be easy to get sucked in by her. She was gorgeous, smart, determined, and able to admit when she was wrong—a trait totally missing in the McCormack genetics—which he appreciated. But this was temporary. All temporary. And he'd do well to remember it. If he wanted to accomplish making a mark for himself, then he had to stick to the rules that had served him so well in the past once his mother had died:

No strings.

No entanglements.

No long-term relationships that could tie him down.

Unfortunately for his sex drive, that included the very sexy Ph.D. he'd be working with in tight confines aboard his ship. He shifted in his chair to ease the pressure caused with the stirring of her sweet fragrance in the air, let alone the image that flared to life in his mind of her in a string bikini. Damn.

He reminded himself that he was a confirmed bachelor. "See you aboard ship?"

She nodded and smiled. "I'm looking forward to it."

He. Was. So. Screwed.

Chapter Three

Bella squinted against the intense sunlight glinting off the azure waters of the Gulf spread out in a glitter-strewn rolling blanket below her. Only the changes in depth that made the blue deeper and the occasional outline of a boat on the water broke up the monotony of the scenery as the helicopter took her closer to her destination.

She shoved her sunglasses back into place with an index finger. "How long until we get there?" she asked through her headset. The humidity and heat in the air were less here than on shore, but still the backs of her thighs were beginning to stick uncomfortably to the vinyl seats of the aircraft. Perhaps shorts, a cropped T-shirt over her swim suit, and flip-flops had been a bad idea, but she figured she was going to be on a boat, so she hadn't worried about it.

The pilot turned his head in her direction, his dark mirrored sunglasses reflecting an image of her. "See that dot at three o'clock? That's the *Discovery*. Ten minutes."

Bella nodded and started scanning the horizon for her first glimpse of the *Discovery*. The yellow and white boat looked small at first, a toy floating in a massive bathtub, but as they got closer, she saw the enormous boom crane off the back and the wide sweep of decking marked for a helipad.

The investor had deep pockets. She sighed with relief. This was no fly-by-night operation. They'd have her skills and the investor's money and a professional salvage diver and his crew. Her heart leapt. This was it. All her dreams and hopes were getting closer and closer. Bella tasted victory in every rapid beat of her heat.

The *Discovery* was a top-of-the-line recovery operation. Judging by the number of decks and the size of it, they had no problem working with a full crew for months at a time without going back in to resupply.

The helicopter touched down light as a dragonfly on the helipad of the ship's uppermost deck. A huge guy wearing Hawaiian-print board shorts and a white tank top ducked under the spinning blades of the chopper and opened her door. Pacific Islander by the look of his squared body, big shoulders, and deeply tanned skin and wide, white grin.

"Welcome to the *Discovery*," he yelled, holding out his hand and helping her down, then taking one of her bags.

The wash of the helicopter props made it hard to hear as she ducked down, and they both hurried out of range of the helipad as the transport lifted up from the deck and darted back into the blue on blue of sea and sky.

She turned to the man and held out her hand. "I'm Doctor Dupré. Bella."

His beefy hand swallowed hers. He had a generous smile, a dark beard, and eyes that sparkled with humor. "Nice to meet you. We've been expecting you. I'm Toneau Lupopo, first mate of the *Discovery*. Let me take your things and put them in your cabin after I show you to the conference room. The captain wants to see you right away. We've been doing some prelim dives with the ROV based on the information you sent, but he'd like to get a briefing complete so we can get this recovery effort moving."

Toneau picked up her bags and started walking. He moved fast for someone who she imagined would have to turn sideways to make it through the narrow corridors down below. They took the teak staircase from the helipad to the deck below, and she was ushered through a set of glass double doors into a sizable air-conditioned conference room.

On one side was a long glass and chrome table with sixteen gray, modern chairs around it. On the other side was a seating area of black leather chairs and couches and a massive large screen television that took up most of the wall space that the windows didn't. Right in the middle was McCormack.

She thought she'd been prepared to see him again. She'd been wrong. All the fluttery expectations and excitement that had been swishing about in her stomach all morning came to an end. Instead, her pulse took over, pounding everywhere until she swore it even beat at the ends of her fingertips and toes. There was something about McCormack that made her go from smart to stupid in seconds.

His build was that of an athlete, and his dress wasn't captain-like at all. His tight black T-shirt showcased his well-defined shoulders and back, and his low-slung black shorts revealed a nice butt, muscular tanned legs, and wide feet in simple black flip-flops. His surfer hair was on the long side and brushed his shoulders in sun-bleached layers. All in all, he looked nothing like his Armani-suit wearing brother or the spit and polish one would expect from the captain of a craft as impressive as this one.

"Captain, Doctor Dupré is here."

His back was to her as he looked out over the water. "Thanks, Toneau. We'll have an all-hands meeting in one hour, then break for lunch."

"Aye, aye." Toneau scooped up her bags and disappeared,

leaving Bella alone with Tucker.

He pulled a remote control out of his pocket and flicked on the wide flat-screen television between them. Cool blue underwater images filled the screen. Soft, rounded lumps and silt-covered shapes appeared and disappeared as the ROV drifted over the seabed. Branches and twigs of straggly coral looked more like tumbleweed strewn across a desert than the bottom of an ocean.

"This is some footage from our prelim dives with the ROV. We've already done three with the coordinates you texted. So far we haven't found anything."

Bella frowned at the moving image. Willing a man-made shape to form on the seabed. "Not even outlying debris?"

He shook his head.

"Before we go any further, I need to clear something up with you that we neglected to talk about in Harold's office."

He turned, his incredible blue eyes sucking her in. His lips curved with a sensual tilt. "You mean the instant attraction between us?"

Shit. Had she been that obvious? That would have to change. Now. Bella swallowed back the retort that rose to her lips. He flustered her, and she didn't want to think about how obvious she must have been for him to notice. She shook her head and tucked her hair behind her ear. "No, actually, that wasn't what I was thinking of at all."

"But you *have* been thinking of it."

She frowned. "Is this going to be an issue?"

He took one step closer. "Not unless you want it to be." His smile got slightly wider, and her heart pounded in response.

McCormack was good looking, but she was not about to let her female Dupré instincts override her own intelligence. She refused to let him keep redirecting her thoughts.

"Did someone explain to you that I'm supposed to take

lead on this project?" she said, her tone matter-of-fact. She hated to jump into this detail, but it hadn't been covered in their meeting in Harry's office, and she wanted to make sure exactly where things stood before the operation got fully underway.

His smile faltered. "So that's how it's going to be, is it? All work and no play?" He nodded. "Okay, Doc. That's fine. I was only told you needed an expert crew to recover a wreck. And since I'm the one with exponentially more experience in the actual water, pulling up items from the sea floor, and responsible for the safety of everyone aboard this vessel, I'd planned to call the shots with *my* divers and *my* crew on *my* boat."

She crossed her arms and took a seat at the table, like she intended to dig in and stay awhile. "But you don't have the historical or preservation expertise."

Wow. The good doctor did not mess around when she went for blood. Fine. If she wanted to go head-to-head, he'd oblige his guest. "True, but now that we know the location of the wreck, once you give us the specifics of what's down there, we really won't need that expertise until we bring it to the surface, now will we? So you can tag along after the initial dive-recovery plan is formed and get some sun while we bring things up for you."

Bella bristled and crossed her legs as well, her foot bouncing, making the silver ring on her second toe wink in the sunlight streaming through the conference room windows. Good. At least now she knew he wasn't a guy to be pushed around just because she had a pretty face. What really amazed him was how she could be so demanding when she hadn't even been on his ship more than half an hour. It concerned him that she threatened the well-run order of his ship. Not every man on board could resist her charms.

"You don't know precisely what you are looking for, or how to catalog, clean, preserve, and store it properly once it comes up," she insisted. "That's my expertise."

He let a slow, almost predatory, half smile lift the edge of his mouth and derived a small sense of satisfaction as the pulse at the base of her creamy throat beat faster. Doctor Dupré still thought she had the upper hand with him, but she didn't realize he'd already discovered two of her vulnerabilities: the wreck and her attraction to him. "Which is why I guess the financial backer wants us working together on this."

"Who exactly is the financial backer on this project? Mr. Palmer was a little sketchy on the details."

She was fishing for answers, which amused him. "If he didn't tell you, then it's not my place to reveal the source." He struggled to keep his expression as neutral as possible.

"But you're friends."

"Close enough that I know him as well as I know myself."

Bella let out an exasperated sigh, uncrossed her arms, and gripped the edge of her seat. "That explains a lot."

His eyes narrowed. "What's that supposed to mean?"

"You think you can call all the shots because you have a doohickey, and I don't," she said, waving a hand in the general direction of his groin.

He paused for just a second and tried not to laugh. "Did you just call my junk a doohickey?"

She glanced down at the floor a moment, a delicious pink color staining her cheeks before her gaze connected with his again. "That's not the point. The point is, I need to be in charge of the salvage. The wreck could be in a delicate state."

She huffed out a breath and leaned forward putting her forearms on her knees, giving him an exceptionally nice view of her cleavage that just about dropped his jaw to the floor.

He'd gone rock hard the moment she'd entered the room, and he'd smelled her perfume—a light, mix of citrus, flowers, and sugar, like *limoncello* sipped on a Sicilian seashore on a hot summer day. Prolonging their meeting one-on-one was just adding to his torment.

Perhaps he'd do best to wrap up their introduction and give himself a breather before he had to talk to the rest of the crew. He forced himself to look at the images on the screen instead of her and hoped his long T-shirt was long enough. If he didn't look at her, perhaps his brain could outpace his libido. He needed to put some distance between them, which on the confines of a ship wouldn't be easy.

"The point is, *Doctor* Dupré, that on board this vessel you will act as a professional and that includes not micromanaging or harassing my crew. I have experience handling a ship of this size. Managing a professional and experienced dive crew. *And* the ship's crew. Ordering and maintaining equipment, purchasing supplies before we need them, and transporting the artifacts back to shore safely. *I* do all that. Plus. Why don't you stick to what you're good at? Cleaning, ID-ing, and cataloging our finds."

He gave her a moment to process that. He could practically hear the cogs in her brain turning. She remained silent. Good. There was only one boss on board, and that was him. If she insisted on pushing, he'd play hardball. He hoped to hell it wouldn't come to that. "We'll be meeting with the rest of the crew in thirty minutes. Please pull together whatever additional data you may have for us to review. It will give us a better scope of what we're searching for before we go down again to set up a sonar scan grid."

She didn't respond, but he could hear her even, shallow breathing. The air held an electric charge that amped up every sense. Just having her in the same space altered everything, like the sensation before a thunderstorm. "Are you on board with that, Doctor Dupré?"

The whisper of movement as she shifted in her chair told him she was no longer seated. He turned and found her chair empty. She was gone.

Thirty minutes later there was sharp knock on her door. "Doctor Dupré?"

The sound of his voice made all the downy little hairs on her arms raise. Dangerous. That's what he was. Just like lightning. She'd seen it so many times before with the women in her family. Men who were in it for the quick hit and then disappeared. Well, no thank you. She was not interested. Somehow she hadn't gotten that message to all her girl parts just yet.

"Sorry, no one is home right now, but we'll get back to you soon. Please leave a message at the beep. *Beep*."

"You have one minute to open this door, or I will." The change in his tone from casual to imperious put her even more on edge. *I will not give in.*

Bella didn't budge from her seat in the cushy chaise in the corner of her room. Why should she? She'd already made up her mind she was finding a way out of this. She would not be conned, duped, or stripped of her legacy because it was a man who claimed he was in charge of the biggest event in her life.

"Thirty seconds." His voice held an edge of irritation. *Good.* He'd certainly irritated her enough. In fact, she was downright uncomfortable around him.

"Ten seconds."

Mentally she did a countdown in her head and stood up to stare out the porthole window in her berth. She fully expected him to walk away. In her experience, men never did what they promised.

After she silently counted down, three…two…one, and didn't hear anything, she felt justified in her assessment and smoothed her damp hands down the side of her shorts.

Then the doorknob rattled and turned, and the door, which she knew without a doubt she'd locked, burst open. Bella turned and stared at the tanned man who filled the doorway to her cabin. "You're late for the all-hands meeting, Doctor Dupré."

"And you opened my door without permission."

He tossed a brass key up into the air and caught it in his hand. "Master key. It lets me in every door on this ship."

"But you can't do that."

"Actually, since I'm the captain, and it's my ship, I can." He slipped the key into the pocket of his shorts and leaned his muscular body against the doorjamb. "I've come to get you. You aren't always late to meetings, are you? It might send the wrong message to the crew."

Bella didn't care for his accusatory tone. She wasn't part of his crew to be commanded as he pleased. She was in charge of this operation. He just hadn't acknowledged it yet. And as of five minutes ago, she'd decided not to attend the all-hands meeting because she had no intention of working with him if he wasn't going to recognize her as the lead on this operation.

The first chance she got, she'd radio back to the mainland and have them send out the chopper. Surely she could talk some sense into Harry, and he could talk some sense into the financial backer. McCormack needed to be advised of his role in this operation and accept it or be replaced.

"Guess you'll have to carry on without me, since, as you so clearly indicated earlier, I'm not really that important to what we're doing here."

A muscle in his jawline ticked. "We can't have the meeting to plan the first research dive without you, and you damn well know it."

"That doesn't sound like an apology."

"Maybe because it isn't."

She shrugged and tried to shut the door on him. Tucker's large hand splayed on the dark teak door stopping the movement, his dark tan looking pale against the even darker wood.

"There's no point in shutting it. I've got the key, remember?"

Bella pinched her lips together.

"What's your game plan?" he said, his tone mocking. "If you think you can run back to your boss and ask him for another dive and recovery crew, you're bound to be disappointed."

She narrowed her eyes. "Really. And you would know this, how?"

"As I said before, I'm a close personal friend of the financial backer for this project. You don't include me in on it, then he'll pull your funding, and no more dive. We're a package deal."

"We'll see about that."

He crossed his arms and leaned his shoulder on the doorframe again, still blocking her only exit out of the tiny but well-supplied cabin. She had nothing to complain about as far as the accommodations.

The smooth wood floors had fluffy area rugs in soft blues, which matched the blue and white nautical theme of the cabin, and there was a porthole window large enough to open and lean out, taking in the beautiful view of endless sea. She had a queen-size bed that she'd discovered was pillow soft when she'd flung herself down on it earlier and a bathroom of her own with marble counters, a radiant-heated floor, and an oversize shower that looked heavenly.

But that angular jaw, those clear blue eyes under dark intense brows, and most of all, that arrogant, smug smile made her do a double take. "Go ahead. Feel free to use the satellite phone. It's over on your dresser," he said.

She would—later. But she wasn't going to give him the satisfaction of watching her do exactly what he said. She'd do it in her own good time. The air seemed to instantly be sucked out of the room by his mere presence. She had no intention of letting him see he'd gotten the advantage over her. Or confirming his suspicions that she found him attractive.

And absolutely, under no uncertain terms, did she plan to jeopardize this operation by getting too friendly with McCormack. She'd been fooled once by Phillip, letting her carefully constructed barriers down around a man from that family, and had paid the price. No, getting involved with another McCormack wasn't worth it. Besides, he may have had that roguish air about him that marked him as different from Phillip, who was more of a corporate type, but that didn't make him good dating material.

He was too laid-back, too much of an adventurer, to ever settle down in one place with one woman, at least that's what she suspected. The McCormacks weren't men to be tied down to anyone for very long. Even his own father and half brother couldn't make do with just one woman. In fact, the only thing she could say that recommended this McCormack over his half brother was the fact that at least Tucker kept his word. He'd said he'd open her door, and he had. That gave her pause. What if he promised other things? Would he keep his word then as well? Just contemplating it made her squeeze her thighs together.

The allure of a bad boy and unlimited freedom to do whatever she pleased was a strong aphrodisiac to Dupré women, but Bella resisted for one simple reason: her family. The small part she had left had to come first. She'd mortgaged everything to make the salvage of the *Rapid* happen, and she owed them the security and respect the find would bring.

"Are you going to make the call and stop stalling this operation, or are you going to hole up in your cabin being self-righteous until your funding runs out? We're on a tight schedule. Hurricane season is coming."

Her hands bunched into fists as she fantasized about punching that smug smile right off his chiseled chin. She hated feeling forced into anything, worse still hated feeling helpless. "I'd be happy to come talk to the crew, once you apologize and they realize that I'm in charge of this operation."

"But I'm not apologizing, you're not in charge, and we both know it."

She took a step forward, challenging him. "You wouldn't be here if it weren't for me."

He gave her a devilish grin. "Ditto, sweetheart. You wouldn't be on my ship, the closest you've ever been to getting your hands on the treasure, if it weren't for me," he shot back.

Everything in her vision seemed to take on a reddish tinge. She hadn't been this upset by a man since Phillip had flipped her world upside down. And in her mind that meant one, and only one, thing. Tucker McCormack was dangerous. "You're wrong about not being like your family." She shook her head. "You're *just* like them."

With that she stormed right by him out of the cabin.

Maybe he was. God knew he had his old man's chin and cheekbones. What else had he inherited that he didn't realize since he'd never really been around his half siblings? Tuck pounded the edge of his fist on the cabin's doorframe. Damn it. He'd overplayed his hand and lost the match.

Bella was not a woman to take orders. It only made her dig her heels in harder like a swordfish fighting on a line. The only saving grace in this situation was she couldn't go very far.

No matter how often she walked away, or which direction, there was no way for her to get off the ship unless she swam or had a helicopter pick her up.

"Cap?" Tuck turned to see Toneau peeking around the corner from the staircase.

"We'll be starting the meeting in five."

"Is the doctor coming?"

"That's up to her."

Humor sparked in Toneau's dark eyes. "Is she giving you a run for your money, Cap?"

"Let's just say she's not making it easy."

"Sometimes the hardest fish to catch are the sweetest to eat," he said and winked.

"Not on this ship. Remind the crew of the protocols. I don't give a damn how attractive the doctor is, there's no fraternizing. Are we clear?"

"Aye, Cap."

He could hear Toneau's heavy footsteps thumping up the staircase to the deck above as he left her cabin and followed Toneau back up to the conference room where he knew his crew was waiting for him. Once Doctor Dupré had time to calm down, perhaps talk to her boss again, then realize she was well and truly stuck with him, she'd come around, and they could get this project underway.

He walked in the conference room, and the laughing and chatter among his crew members died down as he moved to the head of the table and the big screen mounted to the wall. "Okay, we've got a big day ahead of us. We're going to send out the ROV again to look for a debris field to narrow our search pattern down. We're also going to send out two teams to cover more area. Many of you know this could be a potentially big haul for us."

"What exactly are looking for?"

"That's—" He stopped mid sentence as Bella opened the

outside doors and came walking in, backlit by sunlight shining off the water. He coughed to cover the sudden tightness in his throat.

"That's what Doctor Dupré is here to explain to you."

All heads turned as she walked toward him, and for good reason. He'd never seen a doctor who looked this good. And he wasn't alone. He noticed some of the more obvious stares and made a mental note to reinforce with the crew that she was off-limits. Then made another to remind himself a time or two.

Any woman on his crew needed to feel as if she were completely safe, especially when they were working and living together in such a confined space for weeks and possibly months on end. Having a no-fraternization policy just made the boundaries clear and easy for everyone to follow.

"But before we get started, let's do a few introductions. Garvis Barclay, our ROV driver." He looked like a cross between military, with his buzz cut and big frame, and a New Jersey bodybuilder with his deep tan and the carat diamond studs in each ear. "Next to him is Jake Williams, who's our backup ROV driver and sonar tech." Williams and Barclay were like the odd couple. Williams, with his thick-rimmed dark glasses, bald head, and ZZ Top-style brown beard down to nearly his navel, didn't look anything like Barclay, let alone like he could work with him.

"Opposite him is Kylen Scott, our other sonar tech. He'll be handling mapping out the wreck and recording everything we do to satisfy the authorities and historians we're not screwing anything up." Scott looked like he was maybe eighteen, with his farm-boy grin, white-blond hair and blue eyes, despite the fact he was in his thirties. He gave Doctor Dupré a big smile, and she nodded at him.

"The redhead next to him is Rory Guereaux. He'll be your lab assistant and will be in charge of making sure all the artifacts are cataloged out of the storage pods when they come up, photographed, and treated however you see fit." The stocky man, whose freckled skin was burned nearly the same color as his hair, smiled.

"I'm half Irish, half Cajun, so if you need me to tell anyone off for you on this boat, let me know," Guereaux added.

Bella blushed slightly. "Thanks, I'll remember that."

"You've already met our first mate, Toneau. And next to him is Tom Reeves who handles our magnetometer." Tom's dark hair and even darker eyes were his most distinguishing features. He was thin and pale, almost like a Goth throwback. Tuck assumed the guy lived on energy drinks and rarely ventured out of the control room.

"Doctor Dupré is an expert on this particular wreck. She's our antiquities and preservation specialist and will be handling any of the material or data you bring back up with you from our surveys and dives." He took a step back and let her have the limelight.

She glanced at him, her fingers fidgeting nervously with the hem of her T-shirt. He'd never thought of her as the nervous type. For the short time he'd known her she'd always seemed to know precisely what she wanted. Then again, this was important to her. Hell, if what she'd said was true, she'd wrapped her whole life around trying to bring up this wreck. She pinched the small mermaid pendant on her necklace and ran it back and forth along the delicate gold chain around her neck.

Bella swallowed hard, let go of the necklace, and tried to focus on the back of the room, rather than the sea of faces looking expectantly at her, or at the distracting presence of McCormack to her right.

Speaking in public wasn't one of her strong suits. It wasn't that she couldn't do it, just that she preferred not to since she had so little filter to begin with. Whatever was on her mind generally came out of her mouth resulting in a lot of moments where she wished she could take back what she said, rewind it, fix it, and then replay the edited version.

She forced her hands to her sides and lifted her chin. *Deep breath. You can do this.* "Good afternoon. I'm sure that Captain McCormack has explained to you that our project is a historic shipwreck. A brig, one hundred and fifty feet in length with two main masts, an extended gaff off the bow, and a copper-sheeted hull. I've got some images that might help."

Bella pulled the USB drive from her shorts pocket and glanced back to see if there was a video unit attached to the screen so she could show them some of the data and images she'd collected. McCormack took the USB from her hand, the contact of his skin on hers rolling straight through her like a warm beverage on a cold day. Her knees wobbled a bit. The plain royal blue screen behind her transitioned to a black and white ink drawing of the ship she'd found in an archive of early-American naval vessels.

"This is approximately the shape of the ship we're searching for. Prior to the War of 1812 it was used as a merchant vessel but was turned privateer by the captain, looting English, French, and Spanish vessels in the Gulf during the war. From the research I've done, it was said to have a good deal of Spanish silver aboard, as well as several cannons, so a magnetometer survey may be of use in locating the main body of the wreck once we find any outlying debris."

A rumble of excited male voices filled the conference room, and it was only then that she realized she might very well be the only female on board. Her heart pounded a little harder.

Tucker stepped closer to her, and she reactively stepped

two steps to the right to avoid having him brush up against her. He leaned forward, his hands spread flat on the conference table in front of him. "Now that you've seen what we're looking for, we need to get a recon dive in before dinner. We've already seen on the prelim side-scan sonar survey that we're still looking for the outlying debris field. Today we've got Scott and Williams on the ROV team, Lupopo and Barclay on sonar 1, and Reeves and Guereaux on magnetometer. Everyone else is on support. Get your stations prepped after lunch and ready to go. I want everyone on point in an hour."

Chapter Four

The conference room began to empty as men pushed back their chairs and headed either down the stairs or out the double glass doors to their assignments.

Bella caught Tucker staring at her. She turned crossing her arms. "What?"

"I'm kind of surprised, that's all."

She tilted her head. "Why?"

"You made it clear you weren't interested in working with me, then you showed up to the meeting when I haven't apologized yet." He pulled her USB from the port on the video unit and held it out to her.

Bella unfolded her arms and took it. The call on the satellite phone with Harry had been worthless. The contract spelled it out in black and white. She was stuck with McCormack and his crew. And he knew it, which somehow pissed her off even more. "There isn't exactly a taxi to take me back to shore. I'm stuck out here, and I decided that as long as I was here, perhaps something useful could come out of this."

"So you still don't want to work with me."

"Want, no. Have to, yes."

His lips curled into a smug smile that made her want to scream. "You don't have to seem so damned pleased about it." As soon as the words left her lips, she realized how shrewish she sounded and wished she could reel them back in. She was irritated with the situation as much as being forced, once again, to compromise to get to her end goal.

"I'm sorry if this isn't what you expected. I'm not the enemy here, Bella. We're on the same team. We both want to recover what's down there."

She nodded. "True, but I intend to fully participate in this operation. I refuse to be relegated to some consultant or footnote. You may be getting half the credit, but don't forget that everything we find is because of the sacrifice and years I put into locating it." She locked gazes with him.

"Duly noted. Anything else?"

"As a matter of fact, there is." She squared her shoulders. "I still want my apology."

"I've already said I was sorry. Look, I know you're not happy about how this is turning out, but perhaps other things are more important, like getting to this wreck and making history."

She nodded. "True."

"Now, if on the other hand, you wanted me to make it up to you in some other way—"

She stopped him short. "Nothing is going to happen between us, so you can get any ideas of that right out of your head."

He held up his hands, but the outline of the smug smile remained, and she could tell he wasn't taking her warning seriously. "Fine, but don't blame me if you can't handle the sight of me stripping out of a dive suit without your bikini going up in flames."

She sighed. "You really think I can't resist your charms,

don't you?"

He stepped closer, purposely invading her air space. A wave of body heat, seasoned with sea salt, sunshine, and something totally male and way too appealing made her breath catch.

"I don't have to think it, Doc. I *know*."

"You know," she said, her voice heavy with sarcasm.

"Simple science." He reached out, a single fingertip caressing her cheek, brushing back a stray strand of hair and tucking it behind her ear. His voice lowered a fraction making her insides curl with heat. "Your pupils dilate when I get too close. Your breathing changes. Add that to that pink hue that starts to color your skin like strawberries covered in cream, and the way you shiver when I barely touch you, and yeah, I know. Say whatever you want, but there's chemistry between us."

Bella turned away from him and walked over to the window to look out at the sea. Her hands were shaking. "The only chemistry we're going to be exploring while I'm aboard this ship is electrolysis to clean the encrustation off our finds."

"You make cleaning sound so sexy."

"You keep to your part of the operation, and I'll stick to mine."

"What exactly are you afraid of?"

She spun around. "I already told you. I don't trust you. You're a McCormack."

He sighed and shook his head. "My big bro must have been a bigger dick to you than I thought." He looked at her, his eyes narrowing. "He really did a number on you, didn't he?"

She crossed her arms. "I don't think that's any of your business."

McCormack chuckled, stepping closer to her, the presence of him invading her space and making her body tingle. "See, that's where you'd be wrong. You made it my business the moment you stepped on this ship. We have to be able to trust and rely on one another to stay safe out here in the middle of nowhere. We have a strict no-fraternization policy aboard this ship, so you're safe from the crew and from me. And before you go making any more assumptions that could jeopardize this operation, let's get one thing straight, you're not the only person here who's been screwed over by a McCormack. So have I."

His words stopped her, cutting down the anger swelling inside her. She swallowed past the tightness building in her throat as she realized he was right. They'd both been hurt by the McCormack family—possibly him more than her in the scope of things. She had no right to continue to hold his family against him. Hell, she hadn't even really given him a chance.

"I'm sorry."

He held up a hand. "Unlike you, I'm not looking for apologies. I just want to work. How about we get back to business with a clean slate between us? I told you I wasn't like them; perhaps you'll believe me, and we can just start over from square one." He held out his hand. "Hi, I'm Tucker, nice to meet you."

Bella couldn't help but smile. The gesture was juvenile, but endearing. Honest. She took his extended hand and shook it, trying to ignore the zing of energy his touch caused which made her breasts tighten in response. "I'm Bella."

He smiled, and she could sense a shift in the air between them. Rather than the crackle of animosity, there was a spark of something else, something sensual. She had no idea where it might lead, but since they were on the adventure together, she decided she might as well find out.

"You ready to see what's down there?"

"That's why we're here, isn't it."

He laughed. "No, we're here to gain fame and fortune. Are you in?"

"Absolutely."

Sunshine sparkled on the endless flat of blue water. It was hot enough out in the sun that Bella had stripped off the T-shirt over her swimsuit to catch some of the breeze off the water. They watched together at the rail on the edge of the ship as the ROV was lowered by the heavy-duty winch into the blue water lapping against the hull of the *Discovery*.

Unexpected butterflies of anticipation flitted and swooped in her stomach. After having worked and waited for so long, the idea that she'd actually be able to see the wreck via the ROV had her buzzing.

"Sure it's out here?"

She glanced at him. "Considering my ancestor was the captain who went down with the ship, yeah, I'm sure."

"And is that how you came up with the manifest?"

She paused, biting her bottom lip. If they were both coming clean, there had to be total transparency between them. "There is no manifest, exactly."

He crossed his arms and raised one dark brow. "We're doing this on a hunch?"

"No. Like I said, I've done extensive research. He was a privateer during the War of 1812. The cargo changed depending on which ships he took while in route to port. But he detailed several items in his last letter home that alone would make it worth our while. The silver I mentioned in the briefing was confirmed in the port documentation before his last voyage."

Tuck leaned a hip against the rail. "Let me get this straight. We're spending a huge chunk of cash to sit out here and find your great-times-six grandfather's grave and hope it's loaded?"

Bella crossed her arms, then realized in the bikini top her right breast was perilously close to popping out of the little triangle of striped fabric and forced her arms down to her sides. Being close to Tucker made her more aware of her body. "That's one way of looking at it; however, I prefer to take the stance that due to a string of unfortunate events for my family, we have insider information on our side that any other crew searching for the *Rapid* wouldn't."

"I can go with that," he said.

The man Tucker had referred to as Barclay came up the steps to the second deck outside the conference room. "Captain, they're ready to send down the sonar, magnetometer, and ROV. Did you want to watch from the control room?"

"No, patch video through to the conference room monitors. We'll track the team from there. Wait fifteen minutes after the sonar and magnetometer are down and scanning before you send out the ROV to investigate the anomalies we saw in sector G3 yesterday."

Barclay gave a short nod and conspicuously avoided making eye contact with Bella. Maybe news that Bella was off-limits would get around the crew faster than he anticipated.

He turned back to Bella, deliberately walking around the far side of the table, grabbing the microphone remote, and selecting a seat on the opposite side of the conference table so she'd feel more at ease. "You might as well get comfortable. Once they get the equipment submerged, the video link to the ROV camera and sonar images will feed directly in here. I thought you might like to monitor the images with me to see if there's anything you notice that could help narrow our search field."

She hesitated. He saw it in the slight tremor in her hand before she pulled out a chair and sat down. "How many dives have you already done?" Her tone was casual enough, but he knew women well enough to hear the waver in her voice. Bella might want to be all business about this, but she was fooling neither of them.

"So far three with the ROV to investigate areas that looked promising on the side-scan sonar passes. We were waiting to spot outlying debris before we committed more resources to the search. The more information you can provide us, the more effective we can be in narrowing the search grid in this area and finding the main body of the wreck."

As if on cue, the large screen split into black on one side and a black and white image of little black dots on a big white field in the other.

"That's the sonar image. Anything that sticks out of the seabed is going to leave a black mark. Harder objects, like metal, pottery, or rock, will reflect the sonar best. Less dense materials, like degraded wood from the hull, will give off a weaker signature."

For fifteen minutes they sat in silence until the other side of the screen lit up with an image of blue water. In the distance was a swirling ball of silver flashes, as a school of fish moved away from the ROV. As the ROV descended, a curtain of effervescent bubbles obscured their view for a moment. The deeper they descended the deeper the blue color grew.

Tuck activated the mic communicating with the ROV team with the push of a button. "What's our visibility?"

"About a hundred feet, captain."

"Williams, take it down to about two fifty, and start scanning the sea floor along the shelf." He turned to Bella and found her looking eagerly at the large screen in front of them as the ROV dove deeper and the sea floor came into view. "The coordinates you gave us pinpoint the edge of the shelf. We don't know for certain if the wreck is on the shallower plain, or if it fell down to a deeper plateau from storm movement through the area."

Bella tapped an index finger against the surface of the conference table. "I took that into account when I did my calculations. The *Rapid* should be in the shallows. Storms, especially higher level hurricanes, like those we've had in the last decade, should have pushed it in further on the shelf rather than pulling it out into the deeper trench. Are you sure you haven't seen any outlying debris?"

Half of the screen looked as though it were a giant aquarium, a large square of dark blue water. Down this far there wasn't much sunlight filtering through, making everything outside of the halo of light from the ROV look the same ubiquitous blue. There was a silver, shimmering flash as another school of fish darted out of the way of the ROV, a shadow or two of the larger wahoo fish that lingered waiting for prey, and the ever-shifting bottom of the ocean, an unbroken undulating surface that disappeared out of the edges of the ROV light, but little else.

"Barclay, start a sonar sweep on the next section of the grid."

"Aye, captain."

She knew they had a lot of equipment aboard, but she hadn't realized before how high-tech the recovery operation would be. "I bet all this fancy equipment set you back a pretty penny."

He glanced at her and gave a lazy smile. "Right tool for the job makes all the difference. Most of what's recovered these days is in deeper water. You can't count on scuba diving for it anymore."

"How'd you get into this?"

He hesitated, his jaw flexing, and she could tell he was holding something back. "Let's just say I worked my way up the food chain."

Bella wasn't surprised he was so tight-lipped about it.

Considering how he'd grown up, his level of trusting people was probably on par with her own—next to nothing.

For a while they watched the screen in silence, each of them fixated on finding the one thing out of place that might indicate the direction in which the wreck lay. A solid line of dark dots appeared on the sonar image.

Bella sat forward in her chair. "Hey, what's that?"

Tucker tapped his mic. "Williams, pinpoint the image on sonar now."

"Sectors K11 and 12, Captain."

"Barclay, get me an ROV image of those sectors."

"Aye, Captain."

He glanced at her. "You've got a good eye."

"Pfft. Watch a pretty much blank screen long enough, and anything different sticks out like a giant neon sign."

He cracked a grin. "Guess that's one way to put it." He tapped his mic again. "Williams, we have any acoustical images that are clearer of that line?"

"Just a sec." Bella could hear the *click, click, click* of keyboard keys. Her palms were growing damp and her heart beating a little harder. *Please, please, let it be something*, she silently prayed. The sooner they found what they were looking for, the sooner she could restore her and Min's finances, and the sooner she could get out of the way of temptation in the form of Tucker McCormack.

A grainy image of the shape came up on screen. Whatever it was, it wasn't natural. It was too straight to be a rock formation.

"What's the ETA on getting an ROV image, Barclay?"

"Give me five more minutes."

This time when he looked at her, there was a genuine sparkle of excitement in his blue eyes; potent enough it made her breath catch.

"Perhaps your bad luck is finally wearing off," he said. "We may have found the piece we've been looking for."

Chapter Five

Energy zipped and sparked along Bella's nerve endings. Her stomach fluttered in anticipation. She grasped the mermaid pendant on her necklace and pulled it back and forth along the chain. Was this the breakthrough they needed? Was this their first piece of the *Rapid*?

She remembered way back to when she'd been so young that seated on the old davenport at her *grand-mère's* house, her feet hadn't touched the floor. The French-made sofa and chairs had been older than her grandmother even then. Bella recalled how, over hot black tea, she'd begged her grandmother to retell the stories over and over of their family history and the shipwreck.

Even as a child Bella had been fascinated and intrigued by the tales of daring and drama. Her grandmother's stories spoke of great wealth and a family whose standing in the community was unrivaled. And even then—as young as five years old—she'd known that *she'd* be the one to find the *Rapid* and restore the family's fortunes and good name. She'd never wavered. Her entire life felt like a giant arrow pointing to exactly this time and place.

Her heart pounded unevenly against her rib cage, and her eyes burned because she was afraid to blink and miss anything. The ROV circled, the lens zooming in on the raised ridge that was perfectly straight, but not flat. In fact, to anyone else it might have looked more like a blackened, bumpy, encrusted log that tapered narrower on one end.

"A cannon," she breathed excitedly.

"Don't get your hopes up. Reeves," Tucker ordered into the mic. "Get me a magnetometer reading on the object."

"Aye, Captain." The seconds ticked by with agonizing slowness before his voice returned. The ticking sound in the background increased until it became a steady hum. "Looks like metal, heavy iron content."

"What's your best guess given the reading?" Tuck asked.

A few moments of static on their mic had Bella on the edge of her seat. "Possibly a cannon, Cap."

Bella shot him an I-told-you-so look.

"Can you use the blower on it to remove enough sediment and get a better reading?"

"No, it's got too much buildup on it. Looks like we'll have to clean it up before we can really see any detail."

"Mark it, and we'll haul it up after we get a full scan of the site." His blue gaze connected with hers, and his lips thinned as he seemed to read her thoughts. "This could be a cannon from a different ship or not a cannon at all."

Bella refused to let him dampen her hopes or the giddy sensations fluttering in her stomach. This was as close as she'd come, and she wasn't about to give up before they'd even brought whatever it was to the surface.

"Why are you waiting for the full scan before you bring it to the surface?" she asked.

"I want to make sure this is a worthwhile site before I send down any more equipment."

"It seems like a lot of work when you could just take the ROV down and start searching."

He shook his head. "Trust me, this will go much faster and have better results if we take a scan of the site first, and if we find it has potential, get a photomosaic of the site. We'll send out the sonar imaging on a non-disturbance survey of about 80 parallel transit line spaced less than a meter apart at a constant altitude of 2.5 meters over the site. In the end, we should have almost three thousand individual images that the computer will stitch together into one big mosaic. It'll be like looking at a wallpaper of the dive site in total. We'll be able to see where every item is sitting before we ever take the ROV down there."

"And that photomosaic serves as our undisturbed record of the site before exploration."

He smiled at her enthusiasm. "Right."

"But that's brilliant! It'll make the archeological record much more complete."

"Now you can understand that there's a method to my going slow. Sometimes patience is what you need to get the job done right."

Bella's stomach did an odd flip-flop, and she let go of the mermaid pendant. While she didn't know Tuck well, she knew enough to sense he wasn't just talking about the wreck but about the fragile new relationship between them.

There was a strong attraction, but he truly believed that if he went slow enough and kept at it, she'd give in. Well, if that was the case, then he didn't know her as well as he thought. Once she dug in her heels about something, she rarely gave in. She was determined not to involve herself with a wealthy man ever again, and particularly not one from his family, no matter on which side of the blanket they were born.

On the surface, Tucker seemed like the type to let the good times roll. He was relaxed, almost leisurely, in the way he did things, and despite being a bit on the intense side when it came to her work, his lax attitude both intrigued and rubbed her the wrong way all at once. Sure, he didn't have as much invested in finding the *Rapid* as she did, but he took his work seriously. Didn't he?

She was beginning to wonder just how far Tuck would go to get what he wanted. And what did he want? Fame and fortune, he'd admitted. Certainly he wanted her in his bed. He'd made that plain enough with his flirting. But what else?

Only now was she beginning to suspect that the unruffled exterior he showcased under a spectacular tan and easy manner was not the whole story. Tuck might cast himself as a knuckle-dragging Neanderthal, better with his hands than his head, but she knew better. His quick wit and keen intelligence still shown through, like light seeping through the cracks of a poorly constructed facade. So what was he hiding from her? And what would it cost her when she found out? Because Bella knew without a doubt, she would discover what Tuck was hiding. It was only a matter of time. And when it came to her family track record with men, whatever it was wouldn't be good.

"What's our next move?"

He swiveled in his chair to face her. "Our next move is to have a delicious dinner, and perhaps a bottle of wine or two."

"I meant on the project," she said, then realized her voice sounded a bit too stern, even to her own ears.

"The sun is setting. Tomorrow we'll get results from the scan, pull up the tagged object, and see if we can confirm this is the *Rapid*, and if it is, then we'll put acoustical transponders positioned around the site so we have exact measurements of a one-by-one meter grid over the site for the sonar to transverse while it's taking pictures."

"Well before that happens, I'd like to talk to the crew, to let them know what they should be looking for to help us in identifying this wreck."

His eyes grew stormy. "Bella, I appreciate how much work you've done in pulling together the details of this wreck, but you have to stop trying to micromanage my crew. They know what they're doing."

"But I have the expertise—"

"And so do they. You let them do their job so you can do your job. Fair enough?"

Bella stood up from her chair and braced her hands on the top of the conference table. "None of you, not a single one of you on this ship, has as much vested interest in this operation as I do. If I seem nosy or bossy, I have a right to be."

"You may want to be in charge of this, Bella. You may think it means more to you than to any of us, but the truth is we're all in, every one of us. We don't give less than our best as a team. And if you want our best, you need to give those men room to do their job without feeling like there's someone breathing down their necks. I know them, and you don't. Trust me."

Trust me.

There were two words that never should be put together in the same sentence. Why didn't he ask for the sun, the moon, and the stars while he was at it? Every man she had ever trusted, her own father included, had let her down in some fashion. She pushed away from the conference table and turned to walk out of the conference room.

"Bella?"

She stopped for a moment and glanced back.

"Where are you going?"

"I'm going to change for dinner."

"No, you know what I mean. I don't want you harassing the crew."

"Fine," she said, her flip-flops squeaking against the floor as she spun around again to leave.

"You do realize this walking out when you don't get your way is a habit, don't you?"

She froze in mid-step, then looked over her shoulder at him. "What did you say?"

"Since the day I literally ran into you, you've been walking away. Which, don't get me wrong, I don't mind, since you've got an amazing ass, but I can't help but wonder why. What makes running away a better option than working things out, especially since you've got plenty of spirit to back you up?"

She crossed her arms over her chest. "It's easier to walk away than say something I'll regret." *Or worse, do something I'll regret,* she added silently.

"But haven't you ever regretted *not* taking a stand?"

She thought about it for a moment. Yes. There were regrets. Didn't everyone have those? It didn't make her special or any different. She looked up to find he'd gotten to his feet and crossed the room so quietly she hadn't noticed. He stood close enough that she could reach out and touch him.

"Stay. You don't need to change a thing." His voice was warm and enticing, his eyes a blue she could easily drown in if she let go. "Have dinner with me."

"But the wreck—"

"Isn't going anywhere," he finished for her. "Besides, we can't do anything about it until we get the surveys and photos we need completed, and the crew is already working on that."

"Aren't you eating with the crew like you usually do?"

"Not if you agree to have dinner with me."

She glanced down at herself, the neon pink shorts and flip-flops and black T-shirt didn't exactly scream dinner date. But if he didn't care, why should she? This wasn't really a date anyway. Just two crew members eating a meal together. Bella nibbled at her bottom lip as she considered her options and the potential consequences.

"You are still hungry, aren't you?"

"Well, yes—"

"And there aren't a lot of other dining options out this far in the ocean."

She couldn't help but smile. "True."

He picked up the phone and called down to the galley. "I'd like dinner for two and a bottle of wine sent up to the top observation deck lounge area, please." He set the phone back in the cradle. "See, wasn't that easy?"

"For some people, everything seems effortless."

He raised a brow. "You can't be referring to me. I've got the scars and stubby, shredded fingernails to prove I clawed my way to where I am." Tuck stroked his chin, dark with a five o'clock shadow that made him look even more disreputable, more alluring—almost pirate material. "And I'm sure you weren't talking about yourself."

She shook her head and laughed softly.

"No, life hasn't ever handed me anything."

Tuck looked around, took another step closer to her, and whispered conspiratorially, "Which means if it isn't either of us, then it's some other lucky bastard."

He held out his arm to her. "Shall I show you to the upper deck?"

Bella curled her hands around his sizable bicep. Lord, the man was solid. Just being this close to Tucker was a rush she hadn't felt in a long time. Perhaps in protecting herself from getting hurt, she'd also missed out on the opportunity for the heady sensations that only came with risk.

He led her to the steps, and they climbed upward. Even with as much walking as she'd done aboard the ship, she hadn't come up here before. The lounge area was like a small outdoor sitting room with several chairs, a small sofa, a wicker and glass coffee table, and a table off to one corner with four chairs.

Bella leaned her hips against the ship's rail and stared

out at the view. The sunset was stunning. Yellow and orange fire shot outward from the horizon, shattering into a play of coral pink and deeper red on the few clouds that danced at the edge of the sea. Copper light danced on the waves looking like a treasure of new pennies boiling up from down below.

"Gorgeous, isn't it?"

"Doesn't compare," Tuck replied.

She turned. "To what?"

He came up beside her, his eyes intent and focused on her as if there was no million-dollar view on display. Bella's body pulsed with anticipation. His finger balanced beneath her chin and the pad of his thumb brushed her lips. "You."

"Tuck, we can't—"

"You're right. I'm pretty sure this could be classified as fraternization."

She spun around to walk away and slammed her shins on a low coffee table, almost catapulting across the top of it. He caught her and kept her from falling, his hands warm and heavy against her bare arms.

"You okay?"

Bella winced. "I think my pride is hurt more than anything else."

The corner of his mouth lifted in a half smile. "I told you running wasn't the answer."

"Maybe you're right." The pain faded quickly, replaced by something more insistent.

"Are you too injured to dance?"

"No, I think I could manage."

He picked up a remote from the coffee table and the blues beat of zydeco music began to flow through the speakers hidden in the canopy, partially covering the lounge area.

Bella smiled. He held out a hand to her, and she placed her hand palm to palm against his. He pulled her in toward him and then spun her away in a swing-like move. Bella laughed, letting the music flow through her. They swayed together, and he caught both her hands in his, spun her around, still holding on to her, so that his arms were wrapped around her, her back pressed against his chest. The warmth rolling off him spiked a rush of heat in her. For a second, she had to remind herself to breathe.

He spun her back around so they were facing again. "You're a very good dancer," he said. His lips lifted at the edges, a knowing smile. "Good dancer, two doctorates. Tell me, is there anything you don't do well?"

"I don't cook," she said.

"But you're Cajun. Isn't that a crime or something?"

A bubble of laughter swelled up in her chest. "Both Cajun and Creole, but I'm afraid my *grand-mère* was the cook in the family. Aunt Min has gotten better over the last few years, but nothing like my *grand-mère*."

"You miss them, don't you, your grandmother and your mom?"

"Every day. People tell you that it gets easier. It doesn't. Not really. You just learn to live with the loss."

"And let the good times roll when they come."

"*Laissez le bon temps rouler.*" She smiled. "Exactly."

He spun her in close again, and this time she felt the hardened ridge of him, hidden by the long edge of his T-shirt, pressing against her bottom. The song changed to a slightly slower rhythm.

She leaned against the hard plane of his chest, absorbing the solid heat he offered and softening against him. He brought his mouth close, his breath warm in the shell of her ear. "You smell so good, like sunshine on a lemon grove in the Mediterranean."

"Good to know. Now I'll know what to expect if I ever get to visit. I've never been outside of the United States," she said softly.

His hands move to rest on her hips, and he slowly spun her around to face him. Maybe it was habit, maybe it was because it felt so natural to be in his arms, but either way, Bella wrapped her arms around his neck as they continued to sway.

"You know, I could take you there."

She shook her head slightly as she got lost in the blue of his eyes. "I never stray too far from home."

"Maybe you should." His hands slid from her hips to curve around her back, bringing them body-to-body, head to toe. Somehow all she could focus on was his very kissable mouth and the sensations flooding her system.

He leaned forward, his forehead touching hers. "Brace yourself, Belladonna Dupré. I'm going to kiss you," he said, his voice low and husky. Her skin tightened in anticipation, and her lips tingled. He smelled of ocean and salt and sunshine, with a hint of peppermint on his breath.

"Do we dare?" she whispered.

"What have you got to lose?" His lips brushed against hers in a feather-light touch that set her afire.

Everything.

But it was too late. In that instant, nothing else mattered as long as he kissed her.

Every last remaining thought left her mind in a rush as he molded her body to his, and his lips pressed firmly against hers. The weight of his hands on her body and the way he held her let her know that he was totally focused on nothing more than the intimate connection between them.

The slick slide of the tip of his tongue against the seam of her lips brought vivid images of his mouth all over her, the soft way he might nibble the dips and hollows of her body. Her breasts tightened, aching in response. The stubble that darkened his chin lightly abraded her face but wasn't scratching the itch that went farther than skin deep. Bella wrapped her bare leg around his, cradling the hard line of his erection against her belly. She arched her hips into him, letting the hard surface of his thigh rub against her intimately to relieve the aching throb between her legs.

"Captain?"

Bella pushed away from him and turned from the crew member with the dark buzz cut and diamond studs in his ears who'd entered. She didn't want Barclay to see her face, hot now with a mixture of both embarrassment and anger that mirrored the increasing red of the sunset.

What the hell had just happened? And how had she let it go that far that fast? She knew without a doubt that getting tangled up with the likes of Tucker McCormack was a recipe for one thing: heartbreak. Been there. Done that. He was a free spirit, and she was, well, she was rooted in the place her family had called home for generations. One didn't walk away from a history, a lineage, like that. It was too much of who you were, ingrained like a pattern in your very bones.

She waited until she heard the clink of plates and cutlery being placed on the table, and the other man's movements fade away.

"Dinner's ready," Tuck said, his voice low and gentle.

She turned. "What the hell was that, Tuck?"

"A kiss?" He was still close enough that she could see the dark graze of stubble on his chin and the sheen of moisture on his lips. One dark brow lifted as he watched her. A taunting smile tilted his lips, not enough to be cocky, but certainly enough to make her uncomfortably aware that he knew she'd liked his kiss and wanted more.

She closed her eyes. "We can't let things go that way."

"I can change the ship's protocol. You say the word."

"It's not that. I don't do short-term flings."

His brows drew together. "I see."

"We're going to be out here, what—another month,

maybe two? I don't want it to be something where we're in the here and now and never think about where it might go."

"You don't want to know that some guy is already planning on walking away from the beginning."

"Exactly."

He pulled out a chair for her at the table. "I get it, but I don't like it. I've thought you were sexy as hell from the moment you pressed those fantastic breasts up against me and then fell flat on your ass in your aunt's shop, but I understand the hesitation. I'm not exactly the kind of guy you bring home to mom."

She shook her head. "It's not you, Tuck."

He grunted. "Yeah, they all say that."

"Don't get me wrong. You're a hell of a dancer and have a kiss that could shimmy a woman out of her shorts faster than an alligator rolling over in the bayou." She walked over to the table and placed her hands on the back of her chair. "We should chalk it up to mutual attraction that can't go anywhere."

"Wrong time, wrong place?"

She gave a sad nod and glanced at her plate. "I'm not so hungry after all," she said, then jerked a thumb over her shoulder. "I'm going to head back to my bunk." She turned on her heel and walked toward the stairs going down to the lower deck.

"Good night, Bella."

She rested her hand on the stair rail and turned to glance at him. "'Night."

Each step she took down, her feet turned more leaden. She hadn't realized how attracted she was to him. That could be a problem. It was one thing to avoid someone you disliked. It was a whole other basket of beignets to be naturally attracted to someone and attempt to stomp on your instincts. But there was no way out. She'd promised herself she'd never get involved with a guy who would easily walk away again. It hurt too much.

Bella opened her cabin door. She hoped to hell things improved by morning. It was tough enough being stressed about her finances, but when she layered in the grinding hope of finding the *Rapid*, then dumped on a boatload of sexual attraction to the last man she should be interested in, she was on overload. The one thing she had 100 percent control over right now was her own libido. Everything would look more manageable in the morning.

It had to.

Chapter Six

Tuck had hoped to hell things would be improved by morning. He'd sincerely hoped that by the a.m. he'd have lost the twisting sensation in his gut. No such luck. After a restless night, he was only more tightly wound. Everything about the good doctor was getting under his skin. As attractive as she was, he knew better than to flirt with her. Problem was, he couldn't seem to stop himself. One whiff of that delectable combo of tart lemon and sweet sugar that seemed to cloak the air around her, and he was like a kid after an illicit cookie.

She was looking for a guy who'd sink down roots, fair enough, but he didn't do roots. Anything that could tie him down would suffocate him in the long term. He'd seen it happen with his mother. Her vibrancy, her joy for life, had slowly been eaten away by the daily grind of being merely a mistress. She'd never had any kind of security, neither emotional nor financial. Yeah, she'd loved James McCormack, but what the hell had that ever brought her? In the long run nothing but living in poverty with a case of heartache bad enough to mourn herself to death. Her son sure as shit hadn't been enough to live for. Even when it came to living or dying, her married lover had been more important to her than her own child.

Tuck had no interest in love. Sex? Hell yeah. Love. No fucking way. Love was a Venus flytrap baiting you with sweet promise, then sucking the life out of you. In short, something dangerous he could damn well live without. This had never been an issue before, so he wasn't sure why he was even going down that road with Bella. She was permanent. He was temporary. That should make all future decisions a no-brainer. If this was so damned easy, why was his gut twisted with unfamiliar emotions and his brain filled with all things Belladonna?

"So how was dessert last night?" Barclay asked as they prepped the transponders to go down in the equipment baskets.

"You didn't bring us any dessert." Tucker half snarled in reply as he checked the wires for breakage and the long, cylindrical cases for cracks.

"You know what I mean." Barclay nudged him with his elbow and waggled his eyebrows. Tuck had the insane urge to lift him up by his swim shorts and chuck him over the side into the water.

"You and the doc hooking up, Cap?" Toneau chimed in with a broad smile. "She's pretty hot for a smart person."

"We are *not* hooking up. She's here to work, like the rest of you should be." He glared at the members of his crew surrounding him. "So how about we cut gossiping like a bunch of girls and get to it."

"Am I interrupting?"

A long, low wolf whistle, raked over his last nerve, and he threw Williams a death glare. "Not another sound, Williams, or I'll have you scrubbing toilets with a toothbrush." The man nodded.

Tucker turned to face her. The early morning light brought out the red highlights in her auburn hair and exposed the smoothness of her skin. Even without makeup, Bella was a natural beauty. With the addition of a pair of sunglasses, bikini top, and shorts, she was a knockout worthy of a swimsuit calendar. The light shadowed the valley between her breasts, and those long, tan legs were like a sucker punch in the gut. The sweet little bow of her lips, combined with her dark hair pulled up into a messy bun, showing off her shoulders and neck gave him an almost instant case of blue balls. Somehow he managed not to groan and shook off the fog filling his brain, making him stupid. Yeah. No. Not a goddamned thing had improved this morning. Same old, same old. He had the hots. He shouldn't have the hots. She wasn't interested. End of story.

"Morning, Doc."

"Did I miss something?" she asked, pulling down her sunglasses to look at him.

"Nothing important." He threw a menacing glance at the rest of the crew, and they immediately turned back to their work. No doubt listening to every word. Damn. They were worse than a bunch of horny teenagers. "You ready to get to work?"

She pushed her sunglasses back into place with her index finger and put her hand on her hip. "Sure. What can I do?"

How about stand there and let me look at you. No. Focus, he thought then tried to picture images of Venus flytraps.

"We need to load all the acoustic transponders into the baskets for the ROV to transport to the site." He pointed out the yellow and black cylinders with a coated wire cage on one end that were about the size and weight of a big Mag-Lite flashlight. He figured it would be easy enough for her to pack them up without help from him or any of the others. It would also keep her occupied while they calibrated the equipment they needed to triangulate the positions of the transponders signals once they were positioned on the sea floor.

He tried to concentrate on the questions and comments firing off between his crew, but it was difficult. His ears kept filtering out the deeper male voices to fixate on the higher female tones as Bella hummed while she worked. He hadn't heard a woman hum songs like that since his mother, and it both unnerved and intrigued him. It was one of the endearing things he remembered about her. And look where being hooked up to a McCormack had gotten her.

Bella was different than any woman he'd ever been attracted to. She didn't just stand out because she was smart or beautiful, even though she was both. It was more like she radiated an energy that was infectious. Her drive, her sense of purpose and certainty, had already begun to rub off on the crew. They were eager to bring up the treasure in a way that was making them reckless.

Twice he had to remind his crew of safety checks. "You sure we're secure and ready to go?"

"Aye, Cap. Triple checked."

"Are the transponders all loaded on the ROV, Doc?"

"For the fourth time, yes." She turned to Toneau and said rather loudly and probably for his benefit, "Is he always this nervous about an observation dive?"

"No, but Cap likes things done right. You call it nervous. I call it meticulous. You got no worries with him. You know it'll be done right the first time, every time."

He needed to remember to get Toneau a case of his favorite mango soda when he went back to shore. The man deserved it.

"Okay, all hands. We dive in fifteen minutes. Let's get the ROV loaded."

Bella put her hand up to shield her eyes from the growing intensity of the sun. The men guided the huge yellow mechanical boom arm into place. The enormous round magnet on the end lowered slowly until it connected to the metal cage surrounding the ROV with a *clunk*. Slowly, with the hiss and mechanical clicking off the boom in motion, it pulled upward lifting the heavy ROV up and over until it could clear the edge of the deck.

"You're welcome to watch from the conference room again if you like. It'll probably be boring since we're setting the transponders in place today," Tuck said, turning on his heel.

Deflated, Bella crossed her arms and gave him a glare she knew he couldn't see from behind her sunglasses. "Are *you* watching from the conference room?"

He paused, blue eyes deep and hard to read. "No. I'm working from the control room."

What was he hiding, and why was he avoiding her? "Well, then I'll watch from there, too."

"There really isn't any room. We'll have a full crew in there," he said a bit too quickly for her to find it believable. "You'll be more comfortable in the conference room."

Like hell. She already didn't care for the sensation of being alone on a crowded ship. She'd really hoped there wouldn't be any awkward moments like this between them after last night. Apparently she'd used up whatever small reserves of luck she had left. "No problem. I'll watch it from the conference room after I grab something to eat."

She'd never been down to the galley before. Food was always on hand in the conference room or available to be delivered with just a phone call. As she walked down the stairs, the heavenly aroma of real Louisiana jambalaya, filled with the trinity of onion, peppers, and celery spiked with garlic along with the spice of Andouille sausage, and the rich, acidic scent of cooking tomatoes, made her mouth water. She was definitely headed in the right direction.

Bella came around the corner to find a swinging door leading into a bright kitchen filled with gleaming stainless-steel countertops and pristine white cabinets. A massive pot simmered on the stove, emitting a fragrant steam. A solid built man, his dark hair cropped close to his skull, with skin the color of semi-sweet chocolate chips was cutting up vegetables. He wore a yellow collared short-sleeve shirt and white shorts, with a blue apron tied around his middle.

"Your jambalaya smells delicious."

He turned, a wide smile, brilliant white against his cheeks and chin. "You must be the doctor they all been gibberin' about." He wiped his hands on his apron, and then held one out to shake her hand. "I'm Chef Antoine."

Bella took his hand and gave it a firm shake.

"Lawd, you got a grip, girl. No wonder you can make those men shake in their boots." He laughed. "Now what can Antoine do for you, sugar?"

"I thought I'd get a little something to eat. They're getting a dive going. Right now I'm in the way more than helping."

"Hmm," Antoine replied. "Feels that way sometimes, don't it."

"Why haven't I seen you around?"

"Because Antoine likes his kitchen. I don't have any reason to go anywhere else," he said and smiled. His hands moved fast as he diced the vegetables, and Bella was impressed he kept his fingers intact.

"Well, from what I've sampled the last few days, you're very talented. Everything's been delicious."

"Good. Good. Now you said you was hungry?"

She nodded.

"So what you hungry for, sugar?" He stopped chopping and held up his index finger. "And don't be sayin' a man, 'cause you just gonna have to get in line. There ain't no hanky-panky on this boat, Captain make sure of that."

"Oh, men are definitely not on the menu."

He glanced at her and put a finger to his lips. "In that case, I got this friend, Louanne, who might like to meet you."

Bella laughed. "No, I like men just fine. I'm cursed, so they never stick around."

"Umm, umm. Now that is a problem." He picked up the chopping board and slid the vegetables into the big pot with the flat of his knife.

"So what do you suggest?"

"For lunch, or for your man curse?" he asked as he set the cutting board down.

Bella smiled. Her aunt would adore Antoine. "For now, lunch."

"How about we do a bit of both? Food can help heal the soul, you know."

"Now you sound like my *grand-mère*."

"Smart woman. So what's ailing you, sugar? Can't fix you the right food unless I know the condition."

"Confusion, maybe mixed with a lot of doubt."

He hummed for a moment. "That sounds like an egg-salad sandwich with a side of little dill pickles." He bent down and pulled a small saucepan from under the counter and filled it with water.

"Really?"

"Absolutely. Egg salad—part mayonnaise and mustard, egg that's both white and yellow, salt and pepper, totally different. Hell, it's so mixed up it doesn't even know what it is, but still perfect. What could be better for confusion?" He turned and walked over to the refrigerator, opened it, and pulled out an egg carton.

"And the pickles?"

He pulled out jars of condiments and a jar of pickles and

balanced the armful carefully on his way back to his spot near the stove.

"All those sour little nagging doubts. All ugly like, but you still got to like them just the same. There's something satisfying about biting them in half and chewing them down to size."

She smiled. "True. You know, maybe this therapy by food thing ought to be a blog or a cookbook or something."

He chuckled as he plucked two eggs out of the carton. "Lawd no, child. Antoine don't need all that attention. Anybody else could do the same if they'd just sit down for dinner with their *grand-mère* once in a while." He set the eggs in the small saucepan, sprinkled in some salt, and turned on the gas stove, the blue flame licking at the bottom of the pan.

"Tell Antoine what's confusing you."

"Mostly the captain. One minute he's flirting with me, and the next he's arrogant and aloof and trying to avoid me. I don't get it."

"Oh, sugar, if I took even half of what I don't understand about men and put it on paper, then Antoine *would* have himself a book. The thing you got to understand about our captain is he's a troubled soul. Man could eat dirty red beans and rice every night of the week. He don't dare get close to anyone."

"But why?"

"You gonna have to ask him." He pulled out the pickles from the jar with a fork and placed them on a plate, then picked up his knife and sliced them into thin spears. "But I suspect everything he's ever loved has been pulled away from him at one time or another. Makes it hard to trust that love isn't going to turn around and bite you in the ass, you know?"

Leaning over the counter, Bella nodded and propped her chin in her palm. "We've all got family issues."

"True enough," he said as he began mixing the condiments

in a bowl. "But at least we got family. I think he's a lost soul, feels he ain't truly got no one."

She straightened and gripped her hands together. "Family is everything to me. I don't know how I would have survived without my aunt and *grand-mère*."

Antoine pulled the saucepan off the stove and went over to the sink where he ran cold water into the pan until the eggs were cool enough to peel. "Not everyone is so lucky. Man like that, takes a special soul to understand his pain and give him the thing he needs most." He placed the shiny, peeled eggs in the bowl and mashed them with a fork, mixing them with the sauce, and a dash of salt, pepper, and paprika. He heaped the warm egg mix on thick crusts of bread and cut her sandwich in half diagonally, placing the triangles on the plate beside the pickles. He nudged the plate in her direction. "There you go, sugar. Now get outta my kitchen so I can hang up my psychiatrist hat and get back to my cookin.'"

Bella smiled, feeling better already. "Thank you." She took the plate and headed back up to the conference room where she picked out a chair to settle in and watch the show. Truth be told, after the first half hour of watching the ROV move at a snail's pace plunking down one transponder after another precisely one meter apart, she understood why Tucker thought she might be bored. Her eyes were heavy, and lunch had made her tummy full. Perhaps she'd rest her eyes for a moment.

Bella had the sensation of being weightless, floating, arms and legs outstretched, hovering in an endless space of blue. The movement of the water as it gently pushed and pulled her back and forth, like a rocking chair moving with a slow and steady rhythm, was her only clue that she was indeed in water and not in some endless dreamscape. The water was like a bright blue sky overhead, sparkling as streams of sunlight filtered down through the surface.

Peering down, she saw beneath her rainbow-colored clouds of fish, every hue from purple to yellow. Not even natural, but Bella let that slide. It was a dream after all. She knew because she could breathe fine and yet had no dive gear on. Frankly, she was surprised she wasn't nude.

She kicked hard and swam down toward the schools of fish that seemed like an ever-shifting Möbius strip of color and flashes of silver as they moved. As she came closer, she recognized they were cavorting over a wreck nestled in the sand at the bottom. The fish parted for her as she neared them, then, rather than scattering like they should, closed back together after she passed. There beneath her laid the wreck, not covered in layer after layer of sediment, but exposed and dark, the jagged beams of the hull poking up and the copper bottom a pale green patina. All across the sandy floor lay bottles and dishes. There was a table with two chairs set upright as if they'd been placed there, with two full place settings of china and what looked like a bottle of wine.

Definitely a dream.

The fish that formed a colorful bubble of sorts around the wreck parted once more, and Bella saw Tuck swimming down to her, his hand outstretched. He wasn't wearing any dive gear either. Two fish, one black and one white, had separated from the colorful cloud and followed him. When he stopped, they paired up, swimming closer and closer to one another, like they were playing tag, chasing each other's tails in an endless circle. He didn't speak, but instead held out his hand. The spinning fish moved to hover over his palm, moving faster and faster until they became a blur and transformed into a sparkling sphere. Her pulse did a quick uptick as she recognized it as a crystal ball.

For you. Somehow he said the words in her head. She reached for the sphere, to take it from him. The moment she touched it she became locked to it. Apparently so was he; neither of them moved. She looked down and found that now, of all times, she'd decided to make clothing optional in her dream state. But then her dream did the same to Tuck, which wasn't such a bad thing.

He pulled her close, their hands still connected to the crystal sphere, their bare limbs sliding against each other in the water. Tuck used his free hand to pull her close, pressing her breasts against his bare chest. His mouth lowered to hers in a kiss that stripped away every other thought except how good he felt against her.

The next thing she knew, she woke with a start as the beeping sound of the boom crane blared outside. Bella rubbed her eyes and cursed under her breath. "Why do I always get woken up right when it gets good?" She yawned and ran her fingers through her hair, then stood up and headed out of the conference room to the rear deck.

Antoine may make a great sandwich, but she had to remember not to fall asleep on egg salad and pickles again if she wanted to sleep well. She hadn't had such an intense dream in years. Bella shaded her eyes from the sun, long enough to slip on her sunglasses.

Tucker had taken his shirt off. She hadn't seen him bared to the waist before, but the muscular structure that his fitted T-shirts had hinted at had been very misleading. He was not just ripped but rock-hard, cut, and gorgeous. His skin was molten bronze painted over sleek muscle. A dusting of dark hair at the low waistband of his shorts hinted at what lay beneath. He could easily make it as an extra in the next *Magic Mike* movie. Reality far outpaced what he'd looked like in her dream.

She swallowed hard, past the pounding of her heart that

had somehow taken up residence in her throat and squeezed her thighs together to stave off the ache building there. Maybe she'd gone too long without a release. Maybe she was still amped up because of the dream. Maybe Tucker was not just hotter than any guy she'd ever dated, but *way* hotter. The wind caught his longish hair, blowing it back, and for a moment he looked like a pirate, laughing with a crew member as he slapped him on the shoulder.

He turned, and she saw a flash of dark and light on his shoulder, and suddenly the air was sucked from her lungs. How had she not seen the tattoo before? Curious she walked closer to him.

His shoulders stiffened slightly. "So was the show as exciting as I promised?" he asked, his tone casual.

"How many did we put down there?"

"Enough to cover the whole site in a one-by-one meter grid."

"No wonder it took so long."

One brow rose over his vivid blue eyes, and his all-too-kissable mouth she'd been kissing in her dreams drew her attention. "Not everything worth doing results in instant gratification. Sometimes the waiting makes it better."

Her stomach tightened. The heat rolling off him and the scent of sunscreen on his skin was enough to put her off kilter, but her curiosity wouldn't be denied. *He could sure do some damage to your heart, girl.* "I see you have ink on your shoulder. I tend to notice it since my aunt is in the trade. Can I take a better look?"

"Sure." He turned around. Up close, the swirl of black and white of the two koi fish forming the yin yang on his well-defined, broad shoulder was spectacular. The scales of the black fish were shaded with blues and purples so they appeared iridescent like a raven's wing, while the white fish had bits of coral and yellow shading that made it seem both warm and alive. Both were intricate in the detailing. Beautiful. She studied the detail, running her finger along the edge of the design, wishing she had the guts to feel his whole gorgeous arm. And then it hit her like a shot between the eyes. She knew that style, that flow of line—this was, without a doubt, her aunt's work.

Even though she'd never seen Tuck's tattoo, it was vividly familiar. It was the fish in her dream. Her heart beat a little harder. What did it mean? Had this all been a set up between him and Aunt Min? How well did her aunt already know Tuck? Was her dream a warning or an invitation?

"Looks like Aunt Min's work."

A smile tugged at the corner of his mouth. "That's because it is."

"Did you get it that day I bumped into you?"

He nodded.

All her defenses were up in an instant. "Is *this* why you were at Inkspell that day? Or was it to get some information on me and find out what I knew about the wreck?"

He turned, so close to her that she could see the individual golden bits of stubble on his face and caught a whiff of the sunshine, salt spray, and something potently male that cloaked his skin and made her shiver. "I was there for the ink. A buddy of mine recommended her. Bumping into you happened to be a perk."

"Did she know you were in on this recovery project?"

He shrugged. "I think I may have mentioned I was in town for a new job. In all honesty, we talked more about you. She did mention you seem to have horrible taste in men."

Bella frowned, her shoulders growing tense. "Well, she's hardly one to talk. It seems like a family trait." He might bring up Phillip, and she didn't want to talk about her incredibly stupid decision to trust him.

"It's obvious your aunt loves you," he said.

Whoa. Not what she'd expected. She relaxed slightly, but there was no way to completely relax around Tucker. Everything about him constantly kept her on edge and off balance. She was the kind of person who did best being completely grounded, black and white. No gray. And yet everything about him made it impossible for her to keep her equilibrium.

He waited for her to say something, anything, after her touch had pierced straight through him. Just a simple unintentional caress, a sample of her light citrus scent, and his junk was ready to go on a rampage. What the hell was it about her that had the ability to knock him senseless?

There was a pause in their conversation as she looked out over the water. She sighed, throwing a sideways glance at him. "I'm going to head back to shore this weekend."

"Permanently?"

"No, for the weekend. You can't get rid of me that easily."

"I don't want to get rid of you." *I only want to alleviate this irrational and unwelcome attraction I have for you. Maybe a few days apart would do just that.*

He shifted his weight from one foot to another trying to alleviate the physical discomfort she caused him by her mere presence.

"Since our dinner the other night didn't work out so well, why don't you come by my aunt's for dinner?"

Interesting. A change of heart? He doubted it. She wouldn't be taking him to have family dinner if she'd changed her mind about sleeping with him. "You aren't cooking, are you?"

She smiled. "Nah. My aunt is making Sunday dinner."

"You don't owe me anything, Doc. I don't want to intrude

on your family."

"Don't take it too personally. I was being something we southerners like to call polite."

He winced. "Ouch. That was a backhanded invitation."

Bella shrugged. "Whatever you chant, whatever you brew, sooner or later comes back to you."

He launched into a coughing fit.

"You okay?"

"Chant? Brew? You sure your aunt isn't taking a little voodoo work on the side of her tattoo business?"

"I try not to delve too deeply into what Aunt Min does or doesn't do. We have an understanding. She doesn't dig in my graveyard, and I don't dig in hers."

"I take it neither of you have skeletons in your closets then," he said with as straight a face as he could manage in the weird conversation.

Bella rolled her eyes. "It's Louisiana humor. Sorry. I forget myself sometimes, and I know it makes no sense to a Yankee."

Tuck's intuition was screaming at him now, telling him the not so subtle jabs she was taking were a defense mechanism as much as a warning. Bella had walls up. Thick ones. Why, he didn't know, but he was dying to find out. His damnable Piscean curiosity was going to be the death of him one day.

Chapter Seven

The Dupré house nestled in the heart of the French Quarter on Governor Nicholls Street. Its solid white-painted brick facade sat cheek-to-cheek with the buildings on either side and flush against the sidewalk. Tuck figured that, other than a coat of paint now and then, it hadn't changed all that much in the last one hundred and fifty years.

Dark forest green wooden-slated shutters covered the long, narrow windows at street level. The closed shutters formed a protective barrier against the curious gazes of people wandering this stretch of the Quarter. A delicate, lace-like wrought iron balcony stretched out over the sidewalk, offering shade from the late-afternoon heat.

"Are you sure we aren't here too early?"

"She said dinner on Sunday, which means be here at four forty-five because we're sitting down at five p.m. sharp," Bella said as she walked confidently up the street from where they'd parked.

The unassuming dark green front door, with its black, wrought iron knocker led into a white marble hallway flanked by pale lemon-colored walls. A staircase, bracketed on either side by feathery green palms in white pots, spun upward to the right. "This way. Aunt Min will be in the kitchen."

Tuck followed Bella down the long marbled hallway in front of them until they veered off to the left. Min was in the kitchen putting food out on platters.

She turned as she heard them enter. "Good, you're here! Grab a plate, and follow me into the dining room." Neither of them hesitated to scoop up the dishes and follow her through the swinging door.

Enormous mirrors, which stretched from nearly floor to ceiling in ornate gilt frames, lined the left side of the room. A row of French doors flanked them on the right, opening out into a courtyard where palm fronds and bright fuchsia-colored bougainvillea fluttered in the breeze and a fountain bubbled happily.

They sat down at a small table decked out in linen and fine china that was dwarfed by the size of the room. "You'll have to excuse the table," Min said as she snapped her linen napkin and placed it in her lap. "We sold the dining room set several years ago, but with just me and Bella, it seemed silly to keep a table that could sit twenty."

He realized what hadn't been said, that the dining room set had probably been sold for a good deal of money when they'd needed it, but he gave her a smile all the same. "Dinner looks and smells fantastic."

A slight pink color blossomed on Min's cheeks. "I don't often get to cook for company."

"Don't let her fool you," Bella said. "She always cooks like this on Sundays. I'm spoiled."

He laughed. "I don't think our chef can compare to your aunt."

Bella shook her head. "Aunt Min's cooking is fantastic, but don't sell Chef Antoine short. He's amazing." She looked at her aunt. "I think you'd like him. He's got a special gift with food for thought."

Tucker listened to them talk as he ate. The roasted chicken, sharp with the smell of rosemary, the creamy potatoes rich with butter and sour cream, and thin green beans sprinkled with crispy bits of bacon and smothered in garlic and olive oil made his mouth water. Bella and Min chatted away, and Min poured them all a glass of wine. Honestly, he was too busy enjoying the food on his plate to worry much about joining the conversation.

"You know, there's a curse on this family," Min said, heaping another spoonful of potatoes on her plate and trying to draw him into their discussion. "Did Bella ever tell you about it?"

He glanced at Bella and she rolled her eyes and shook her head, even though her lips curved. "Ignore her," she mumbled.

Tuck couldn't help himself. Min had awakened his curiosity, and it wouldn't rest. "Curse, huh? That explains some lingering questions."

Bella gasped and prodded him with her elbow. He laughed in response.

"It all started when the sea captain of the ship you're salvaging, Pierre Dupré, was caught up in a marriage he couldn't stomach. He had a dark mistress, not uncommon in those days, but it angered his wife, and she made things miserable for the girl. She didn't know the girl's mother was kin to a voodoo priestess of some regard. Story is, she put a curse on the Dupré family that no man would last with a Dupré woman in his bed."

"So you're telling me there's a history of erectile dysfunction in the family?"

Min laughed. "No, sorry, it would be easier if that were the case. No, they either leave, or they die. Either way, they don't stay long."

Interesting, and certainly supported his Venus flytrap theory about love. Maybe he was blowing this out of proportion. While he knew he could be perfectly comfortable having a physically satisfying relationship with no strings attached, he knew Bella wasn't into scratching an itch and moving on. She wanted to entangle herself in someone's life, like kudzu winding with tenacious vines that overtook everything. The problem was, as long as they were in close quarters together on ship, he was sorely tempted to seduce her anyway.

"Is this really suitable dining room conversation?" Bella said pointing a fork at her aunt. "I remember someone who would have made me go wash my mouth out with soap for bringing up death and voodoo in the same conversation at Sunday dinner."

Min picked up her glass of red wine and took a healthy swallow. "True, but your *grand-mère*, God rest her soul, isn't here, and he might as well know the challenge he's in for."

"Oh, I don't think Tuck is planning on sticking around long after the salvage is finished," Bella said.

Tuck chuckled. "It's only a challenge if you accept to run the gauntlet."

"Also true." Min saluted him with her glass and took another drink.

"For curiosity's sake, how is the curse supposed to be broken? There's always a way break these kinds of things, isn't there?" he asked.

Min circled her finger around her crystal glass making it ring out a clear, pure note. "As a matter of fact, there is. And I suspect it's part of the reason our Bella is so keen on finding the treasure Captain Dupré lost so long ago."

He glanced at Bella, and she raised one dark, sleek brow in challenge.

"Really? Tell me more, because I think she neglected to mention it on her initial report on the ship."

"It's nonsense, really," Bella said. "There's this wiggitywhack idea that if the crystal ball he'd bought for his mistress ever made it to New Orleans, the curse would be broken. It never made it. So the curse is still in play." Tuck set his fork down. He knew Bella and her aunt were a bit eccentric, but he'd taken Bella at least for being a logical, rational woman—not a woo-woo believer. "A crystal ball? Seriously? That's all she wanted out of the deal?"

"Oh, it wasn't any crystal ball," Min said, refilling all of their glasses. "According to the legend, it was made from a fist-sized diamond."

This time his mouth dropped open. A diamond as big as his fist? Was she kidding? If the story was true, it would be worth *millions*. Now Bella's interest made sense. She was practical and logical after all. With something that valuable waiting to be claimed, his interest in the wreck took on a new depth. If he could secure the diamond crystal ball, he would have the means to buy out the McCormack company holdings outright, rather than take it down piece by piece as he acquired the funds.

Bella's gaze connected with his. "Now you know why there was no reason to mention this silly family story. It's highly unlikely that this thing—if there was even a crystal ball in the first place—was a *diamond*. And if it was, it's probably not even down there anyway."

"But what if it is?" he said pointedly. "Were you hoping I'd mistake it for a run-of-the-mill historical find?"

Bella leaned back in her chair her expression turning sour. "*Crystal ball* is on the list I gave you. Look it up. It's not like I've hidden this away from you."

"But you still don't trust me," he shot back. "Not enough to tell me this side of the story, anyway."

She shrugged. "No, I don't trust it enough to base my professional career on it. I'm a scientist and historian. It's a family fairy tale. Who's to say it's even real? Maybe the mistress made it up to scare men away from the Dupré widow."

"Well, it scared more than just the men away," Min said flatly. "That's when our fortunes began to take a turn. It took several generations for the wealth to peter out completely, but I'm not sure there's been a man for generations, besides brothers, who've stayed connected to this family for longer than a few years."

"Good thing I don't believe in fairy tales, then," he said. "Who knows, maybe with the find of the *Rapid,* your family's fate is about to change."

Min raised her glass. "I think a toast is in order. To the crew aboard the *Discovery*; may they discover a way to change both our fate and our fortunes."

Bella lifted her glass and so did he, touching the crystal glasses together so that they rang out like a bell.

"I'll drink to that," he said. He took a swallow then set his glass aside for a moment. "So what are you planning to do, *if* we find this crystal ball, and *if* it actually turns out to be a diamond?"

Bella rubbed her glass with her thumb and sat back in her chair. "Well, I might put it on the fireplace mantle."

He gave her an incredulous look. "Really? I can think of a lot better uses than that once it's broken the curse."

She took another sip of her wine. "In all honesty, once I pay off our debts from selling any of the other finds we make, I'd like to give something back to the city."

"You mean like a charity or something?"

Her eyes narrowed as she thought. "No, more like a museum. Something that could bring tourists to the city and at the same time celebrate our heritage."

Min nodded. "Makes sense. I swear I'm the only woman in this family that's ever lived outside this place since we got here when it was still a colony."

"I even saw this building down by the waterfront for sale across from the original Café du Monde that would make a fabulous location," Bella said. She shook her head. "But that's a pipe dream. Right now, we've got to see what's even down there."

They all sipped their wine, and Min looked over at Bella. "So tell me how things are going. What have you found so far?"

Bella's eyes lit up, her enthusiasm making her practically sparkle. How Phillip could have been stupid enough to let her get away, he had no idea. She was beautiful, levelheaded, and smart. In fact, come to think of it, perhaps having Bella by his side would be the icing on the fuck-you cake he planned to give his half brother. Not only would he lose the family company, he'd see the sexy-as-hell woman he'd been too short-sighted to keep on his bastard brother's arm.

There was only one problem with that scenario, sweet as it was. Bella would have to *want* to be on his arm. She wasn't some airhead reality starlet to be toyed with. She wouldn't be in any kind of relationship with him unless she truly wanted to be. Perhaps he was going to have to work harder at gaining her attention and even harder still to get her to see the sense in selling the crystal ball, if they found it. But that would have to wait. For now, he enjoyed listening to the two Dupré women talk with excitement. Bella told Min all about their finds of the last few weeks, while the utensils clinked on the china as they ate. They laughed and talked, filling in the space.

There were no awkward silences or grim stares at this table. Frankly, he envied the easy flow of conversation and shared inside jokes between them. That was something he'd never had with anyone besides his mother and one or two close friends. For him, family meant him and his mother, just the two of them.

There had only been one or two family dinners with his father present that he could remember. Both times he'd felt the heavy stare of his father on him, as if the man expected something miraculous to happen as he ate his dinner and tried to remember to sit up straight in an uncomfortable collared shirt and stiff slacks and keep his elbows off the table and his mouth shut unless spoken to. His mother had expected him to be seen, but not heard.

"You enjoying that chicken?" Min said as she pointed a fork at his plate and smiled. "You've been awfully quiet, so I'll assume it's because my food is too good to stop eating for conversation."

He returned her jovial smile with one of his own. "Definitely the best meal I've had in years. Nothing beats a good home-cooked meal."

Bella made a derisive noise.

"Now I know you didn't make that noise because you don't like my cooking," Min added, looking pointedly in Bella's direction.

"No, you know I love it. It's just I find it hard to believe that with as much world-traveling as Tuck's apparently done, and given the chef on his crew, he hasn't run into any food finer than a regular Sunday night supper at the Dupré house."

"Then maybe it's the company as much as the food," he said and winked at Min just to piss Bella off.

Bella sighed and rolled her eyes. "Could you lay it on any thicker without a shovel?"

"Belladonna Dupré, that is no way to talk to a guest at our table," Min said, her tone reprimanding and jovial at the same time. "Besides, maybe I enjoy a little male flattery now and then from someone so handsome."

Bella gulped back a drink of wine. "I don't understand

why you take him seriously. He doesn't even take himself seriously."

Min's penetrating green eyes focused on him, sifting through his soul like a douser looking for water. "Maybe that's because this poor boy never got to have much fun when he was a kid, Bella. Can't blame him for seeking it out as a man."

An awkward moment took over, where they were all silent, chewing sounds and the clinking of silverware the only things accompanying the radio softly playing eighties rock in the background.

"When was the last time you had dinner with your family?" Min's question couldn't have been more pointed.

He shifted in his seat under the scrutiny of both women looking at him, expecting him to fess up to something he simply didn't talk about. With anyone.

"A very long time ago. Probably before junior high."

"What?" Bella said, then stared at him. "You're kidding."

"No. My father wasn't exactly the family type, at least not with my mom and me. I think he saved that up for his other kids."

"What about your mom? Surely she had family dinners with you," Min said.

He shrugged. "When she wasn't pining away for him, or with him, we ate together, but it was usually takeout or fast food. Cooking wasn't her strong point."

"Didn't you spend any time with your father?" Bella asked.

"He came over for dinner once or twice when I was a kid. Most of the time he didn't show up until I was already in bed. I could hear him and my mother laughing together and doors closing, but not much else." Tuck stopped himself. Why in the hell share this with her? Maybe it was the wine Min had served. It was damn good, and he'd had several glasses.

"But your dad obviously loved you. I mean, why would

he provide for you and your mom if he didn't care? He could have just walked out on both of you. That happens often enough. Take it from a girl who knows."

Tuck set down his wineglass, aware that if he gripped the slender stem any tighter he might snap it in two. "Guilt, plain and simple, and probably a dash of pride. He didn't want it spread around that his illegitimate child was an idiot—might have reflected badly on him—so he paid for me to go to school. He made sure I had tutors, then private school after third grade where most of the kids were shuttled there by their nannies or chauffeurs. Turns out a lot of them saw their parents less than I did, so not seeing my father was normal to them."

"But you still lived at home and saw your mother, didn't you? At least you had that family," Min said.

"I did, until junior high. By then, dear old Dad thought having a mistress with an older child was a bit of an inconvenience, so he had me sent away to boarding school in Switzerland."

"And your mom let him?" Min said, crumpling up the napkin in her hand.

"Oh, she not only let him, she applauded it, because I was going to get a first-rate education at some of the finest schools in the world. I got to see her on holidays, but that was about it."

No one had come to his high school graduation, because it was too far away and too inconvenient. For many years his ambition had been to earn his father's praise and approval. It had never come. By his freshman year at an Ivy League school, his father had passed away, leaving him and his mother on their own again, without the benefit of his financial support.

"But your father sent you to college," Bella said.

"He did. Then he died. And once he died, his legitimate son, as the executor of his estate, decided he didn't like a trust fund going to the mistress and kid who'd made his and his mother's lives so miserable, so he had it legally cut off by putting a rider on it."

"You mean like a certain age?" Min asked.

"No, more like a certain number. The value of the trust is ten million. He set it up so I can't touch it until I match what my father left for me."

"Match? Ten *million* dollars. That's ridiculous!" Bella fumed.

He shrugged. "It is what it is." With hard work and savvy investments, he'd passed that marker less than a year ago. He refused to touch the trust. It was like blood money, his mother's life put into a monetary value. Unfortunately, he didn't have enough yet to buy out the McCormack Group valued at forty million.

"How can you be so casual about it? God, Tuck, don't you ever get worked up about anything?" she said sharply.

He grabbed hold of the wineglass, and took a drink, trying hard to swallow down the mix of emotions swirling in his system down deep so they wouldn't well up and spill out.

"I learned a long time ago that getting worked up over things I couldn't change wouldn't get me anywhere," he said as he swirled the dark red wine around in his glass. "Focus and drive are way more helpful. And for focus, you need a calm head. For drive, you need clear thinking." He looked at Bella and took a sip.

"But matching that enormous amount isn't even possible."

He gave her a crooked grin. "Anything is possible, Bella. It only depends on how badly you want it."

She slipped her hand into his and gave it a squeeze. Sure, it was sympathy, but right now holding her hand made things better.

The thumping of the ancient doorknocker echoed off the plaster walls and marble floor in the front entryway. Bella turned to her aunt. "Did you invite someone else to dinner?"

"If I did, they're about an hour too late," she said and tossed her napkin on the table.

"I told Toneau we'd be here if the crew needed to find us."

"Then maybe it's someone from your work. Personally, I'm hoping it's Publishers Clearing House, and they've got an oversize check. Sit. I'll get it," Min said. She headed out of the dining room to answer the front door.

The sound of a muffled male voice mingled with Min's higher feminine tones, and the two became louder as two sets of footsteps approached the dining room. Immediately Bella dropped her hold on his hand and pulled both her hands into her lap, folding them tightly together.

What the hell?

Bella would know that voice anywhere. Jackson Palmer, her boss's son. Of all the craptastic timing. She decided fate was being a serious pain in the ass tonight.

Her ear caught the slightly irritated quality of Min's voice, but she doubted that Jackson even noticed. He was kind of dense when it came to picking up signals. She'd already told him several times before that she wasn't interested in dating him, but he wouldn't take the hint. Until this point, it had been a minor annoyance, but him stopping by like this was taking it too far.

He and Tucker were probably as polar opposite as one could get on the potential dating pool scale. Where Jackson was naturally amiable and clueless, one always got the sense from Tucker that he was a step ahead, his wit sharp, and his comments even sharper. More than that, Tucker had the air of being a shark beneath the water, powerful, lethal, and not to be messed with, while Jackson was more like a goldfish, happy to swim in circles in the same small bowl until a meal came along. Which, come to think of it, was probably why he was here.

Aunt Min always was punctual about dinner. She was a free spirit in many ways, but there were a few family traditions she clung to, and one of those was Sunday dinner, promptly at five. Without even meaning to, Bella noticed she'd leaned away from Tucker at the sound of Jackson's voice. He strolled into the dining room with Aunt Min, a bouquet of yellow roses in his hand, and all smiles until he saw there was another man in the room. The edges of his smile faltered.

"Hey, Bella, I heard you were back on land for a bit, and I thought I'd surprise you. Sorry, didn't realize you'd have company."

"Jackson, this is Tucker McCormack," Aunt Min said, quickly stepping into the awkward opening in the conversation. "His crew is working with Bella on the salvage of the *Rapid*."

Jackson gave a quick, curt nod to Tucker. "Oh right, the salvage operator my dad mentioned. Nice to meet you. I'm Bella's boyfriend, Jackson Palmer."

Bella's stomach dropped as she watched that keen gaze she knew so well take in Jackson and measure him without the man even realizing it. Tuck extended a hand, apparently deciding he wasn't a threat. "Nice to meet you."

Tuck threw her a questioning look that she easily interpreted as *what the hell?*

She glowered at Jackson. "You are *not* my boyfriend. We aren't even dating."

"Aren't these beautiful?" Min grabbed the flowers from Jackson. "I'll put these in some water. I think there's some dinner left in the kitchen. Let me get you a plate," Min said, smoothly leaving Bella alone in the room with two men who were sizing one another up like two dogs with one bone.

"Bella's something, isn't she? I bet she's keeping your crew on their toes."

"Yes, she certainly is. She's full of surprises," Tucker replied.

Rather than have them continue discuss her like an artifact from a dive, she pushed her way into their testosterone-fueled exchange.

"Would you two excuse me for a moment?" Belatedly her manners kicked into gear. "Jackson, can I get you something to drink?"

He glanced at Tucker. "A glass of wine would be nice."

"Coming right up."

"You wouldn't mind getting me another glass, too, would you?" Tucker drawled and held out his glass to her.

"Sure." Bella poured some wine in his glass and then a glass for Jackson, but found when it came to her own glass there was only a sip or two left. Damn, just when she could have used it. She held up the bottle. "Be right back. Need to get another bottle," she said as she headed for the kitchen.

She pushed on the swinging door so hard it almost slapped her in the butt on the rebound. Min was humming to herself, a perfect plate of dinner in one hand and a cake stand, with a frosted lemon cake balanced on top in the other. The roses from Jackson were artfully arranged in a cut glass vase.

"Here, let me get the cake," Bella said.

Min's lips twitched. "Getting a little warm in there for you?"

Bella bit her lip. "You should see the two of them in there, sizing one another up. As if I'd even consider dating either of them."

Min shrugged. "It's what men do when they are in competition for the same woman."

"They are not in competition over me."

"You sure about that, *cher*?" Min set the plate and cake

stand down and rested her lower back against the countertop. "Because from where I've been sitting, Tucker has been sending a whole lot of signals your way that he's sweet on you."

Bella sighed. "He may be sweet on me, but I'm looking to settle down and he's not. End of story."

"Is it? The way I see things, you two are closer in a month than you've been with any other man I've seen you bring around for dinner."

Which, in all honesty, was only two, Bella thought. Not much to compare to. "So when were you going to tell me you did his ink?" she said, trying to change the subject.

Min took a knife from the drawer and started to slice the cake into thick, pale yellow wedges releasing a pleasant citrus scent into the air. "When you asked," she said, smoothing her finger along the blade of the knife and licking off the cream frosting. "That boy has potential, you know. I can see it in his aura."

Bella groaned. "That's not even possible." She pulled another bottle of wine from the cupboard and picked up two plates with cake. "So how'd you settle on his design?"

"He picked it. Says it represents his sign."

"Fish?"

Min shook her head. "Pisces."

"Explains why he's so at home on the boat," she muttered.

"What's really troubling you, *cher*?"

Bella locked gazes with her aunt. "I saw his tattoo in a dream."

"Not surprising since you've been around him. Maybe it's your subconscious trying to work on the attraction you say isn't there."

"No. I saw the tattoo in my dream *before* I saw it on him."

Min's eyes widened a little. "Really, well that *is* interesting."

"For once in your life could you be less cryptic? Throw

me a bone here. What the hell does it mean? Is it a warning to stay away from him or an invitation?"

"Depends on the dream, *cher*."

Bella repeated the dream oddity by oddity, trying hard not to leave any detail out.

"And the fish turned into the crystal ball?"

Bella nodded. "That's what it looked like."

"Hmmm." Min took a swipe of the frosting on the lemon cake with her finger and licked it off. "Sounds like a sign to me. Maybe he's the one who's going to break the Dupré curse."

"I don't need a man for that. I can find the crystal ball and do that myself."

Min smiled. "If you say so, *cher*, but I've found having a man for certain things makes it infinitely more interesting."

Bella huffed and looked at the roses. "What on earth is Jackson thinking? I've already told him I'm not interested."

Min laughed. "Jackson is used to getting his way. I'm afraid his mama and papa spoiled him. No is simply an invitation to try harder."

"So what am I supposed to do?"

Min's eyes sparkled. "Well, now if it were me, *cher*, I'd let him see you're already taken. That might be the only way to get through to him."

"And I'm supposed to do that how?"

"Let him believe you and Tucker are an item."

Bella thought on that for a moment. "Huh. That might work."

Min picked up the other two plates of cake and gestured to the dining room. "Shall we serve dessert? I'm sure those boys are wondering where we've run off to."

Bella sighed. "Might as well. Can't let your lemon cake go to waste. That would be criminal."

The two women entered the dining room and passed out the cake. Bella uncorked the wine, refilled the glasses, and sat down again next to Tucker. Beneath the table she rubbed her leg against his. She felt the muscles of his leg harden for a moment. His gaze caught hers assessing her, trying to read her intent.

"How close are you to bringing up the treasure?" Jackson asked between mouthfuls of cake.

"We're still in the early stages," Tucker answered, and as he talked his hand found hers and his thumb stroked the inside of her wrist, sending a cascade of shivers through her. "It could still be months before we have much to show for it. We'll be out at sea for quite awhile yet." He threw a warm glance in her direction that shot all the way through to her toes.

"Y-yes," Bella stammered. "We've barely started." Bella leaned over and lightly kissed Tuck's neck just below his ear.

Jackson frowned. "Oh. That's kind of disappointing. The way my dad was talking about it, you practically had your hands on it." He stabbed at his cake and took another mouthful.

Bella cut off a bit of the cake with the edge of her fork and took a bite, very aware of the pulsating heat radiating from Tuck.

"You've got a bit of frosting on your lip," Tuck said. She glanced at him, their gazes locking, the same moment he brushed his thumb slowly and gently against the corner of her mouth, and Bella's body throbbed in response. Who knew eating cake could be an invitation to seduction?

She swallowed hard. "Thanks." Her voice sounded breathless to her ears.

Silence penetrated the room for a moment. Bella could hear nothing but the pounding rush of her heartbeat.

The corner of Tucker's mouth lifted a little in a knowing half-smile and he turned back to Min and Jackson. "In fact, we've got to be getting back soon. They should have completed the scans we need, and I can't wait to see where they'll lead."

"Yes, we should be getting back," Bella echoed.

"Thank you for the fantastic dinner, Miss Dupré." Tuck stood, and taking Min's hand, kissed the back of it.

Min smiled and rose to see them to the door. "I'm so glad the two of you could come."

"Nice meeting you, Jackson," Tuck said over his shoulder.

"So I'll see you. We'll make plans for later then," Jackson called out as they headed to the front door.

"We'll see," Bella said.

The front door had barely shut behind them when Tuck pinned her against the cool brick wall with his arms braced on either side of her. "What are you playing at?" His eyes were bright and intense.

"Who said I was playing?"

"Admit it. You were trying to throw Jackson off. I could tell something had changed the minute you came back from the kitchen."

"Maybe at first it was to give Jackson a reason to back off, but then he couldn't see under the table, so that part had nothing to do with him."

"Do you know what you're asking for?"

Did she? Her heart was thumping hard against her ribs and her breasts aching to be touched. Hell if she knew. Maybe for once she'd put things in fate's hands and see what happened. "Let's find out."

Chapter Eight

Apparently he was done flirting with her. Tuck leaned in and kissed her hard. Bella's entire body responded to the heady invasion with a raw, needy edge. He wrapped strong hands on either side of her waist, then skimmed them down to trace her hips, drawing her closer until her belly pressed against the hot, hard length of him, and the core of her throbbed in response.

She could sense the hunger in him, the need to be her sole focus, the reason she breathed. And regardless of her uncertainty, she couldn't help sinking into the sensation and letting it wash over her. Even as his teeth grazed over her bottom lip and his tongue slid against hers, she still wanted more. Bella wrapped her arms around his neck, fingers tangled in the hair at his nape.

Only the sound of footsteps from inside the house coming toward the door made them pause. Both of them were breathing hard, air sawing in and out. "This way," she said breathlessly as her heart pounded erratically, and her lips buzzed from the kiss.

Grabbing his hand, Bella pulled him along the street to the far end of the house. The streetlight illuminated the street but didn't reach beneath the balcony, leaving them in the dark. Fortunately, she didn't need the light to tell her where she was. She undid the wrought iron gate that had once been the passage for horses and carriages to get to the stables at the back of the property. She refastened the gate. They hid in the shadows, his body, solid and warm pressed against hers as they stood face to face.

The night air was humid and warm, scented with the jasmine that grew up and over the garden walls at the other end of what she'd always called the tunnel. Built for carriages, not cars, it was as narrow as a parking space, which meant Tuck seemed to take up even more room. The plinking, repetitive sound of dripping water from the air conditioner at the back of the house echoed off the brick tunnel walls.

This close and personal, Tuck's signature scent of clean male, ocean, and sunshine, blended with a hint of coconut sunscreen, surrounded her. The scent reminded her of the open sea, big blue skies, and beaches of powdered sand.

"Shh." Bella pressed an index finger to his lips. The blue depths of his eyes filled with a spark of mischief. His mouth twitched.

"What would you do if I made you scream right about now?" he whispered.

"Never let you touch me again," she said. The edge of her tone was pretty much lost because she was trying not to be heard. "Quiet!"

Right around the corner, not five feet away, the front door opened, and the voices of Jackson and Min punctuated the hot, humid night air. Tucker bent down farther, nuzzling her neck with his soft lips. His kisses made her knees weak, and she had to grab his upper arms to hold her upright. Her aunt and Jackson carried out a prolonged version of pleasantries as they said their good nights. Bella wished they'd get done already. She didn't like the idea of being discovered by Jackson. It would be both embarrassing and probably wound him unnecessarily.

"You smell so good, and you taste even better." Tuck's barely audible words were hot in the shell of her ear.

Bella tried to pay attention to what was going on around the corner, she honestly did. But with the onslaught of Tuck's kisses and the sweep of his hand beneath the edge of her shirt, his work-rough thumb grazing against the edge of her ribs, she couldn't focus on anything but him.

The only thing that snapped her out of the sensual haze was seeing Jackson walk by out of the corner of her eye. Her brain finally engaged long enough to take back her body.

"I think he's gone," she whispered.

"Good." He pulled back a fraction. "All the better to kiss you."

She put her hands flat against his chest. "We ought to be getting back to the ship."

He grumbled something under his breath, closed his eyes and nodded. When he opened his eyes again the fire of desire had faded to a smolder. "You're right. I let myself get carried away. It won't happen again."

His words stung. She hadn't meant she wasn't interested, rather that here was not the time nor the place for them to get so carried away that they didn't pay attention to what was happening around them. "I didn't mean—"

He cut her off and pulled away from her. "Look, I get it. You were putting on a show for Jackson, and I got carried away. No harm, no foul."

"You know, if you could let me finish my sentence before you finish it for me, it would really help."

He stared at her for a moment. "What else is there? You already told me you don't intend to get involved with something that's just temporary. I knew it. But when you offered, I thought you'd changed your mind. Now I know better."

She nibbled at her bottom lip. Half of what he was saying was the truth, but the other half wasn't. "It's a woman's prerogative to change her mind."

He leaned in, enough to make her heart beat harder in response. "And have you?" he asked, his voice raspy and hushed, the sensual words of a lover.

Her natural instinct was to dig in, shut him down, prove she didn't need him or any other man, unlike the Dupré women before her. But the temptation he offered was almost impossible to resist. What would it hurt if she changed her mind? She could always change it back again, couldn't she? "I'll let you know once we get back to the ship."

He insisted on driving her car back to the dock and drove much faster than she normally would. With minimal conversation, they took the helicopter back to the *Discovery* bringing with them some supplies the crew needed, as well as a cargo load of uncertainty for both of them.

Bella was still all jumbled up inside. Tuck hadn't been wrong about the inherent chemistry smoldering between them, but it still didn't mean getting together was the *smart* thing to do, at least not in the long term. Bella knew if she slept with him, she would give away a small piece of her heart. She couldn't help it. It was how she was wired. She also knew he would walk away. That's what the men in her life always did, and Tuck was on track to be no exception. Sleeping with him meant inevitable heartache, but sitting next to him in the helicopter, she had to admit that perhaps the pros outweighed the cons. She was beginning to care less and less about the heartache and more about satisfying the real ache of need he'd teased out of her.

Dusk was taking over the sea and skyline, casting the

world into a play of light and shadow. She stared at his profile, the straight line of his nose, the strong edge of his jaw, and the tempting curve of his lips. Falling hook, line, and sinker for Tuck was the easy part. Surviving it when it all fell apart was the part she wasn't sure about. And yet, why had she had the dream? It had to mean something, didn't it? Her aunt certainly thought so.

Tuck didn't wait for the helicopter to fully touch down before he hopped out. Seconds later when she felt the skids hit the helipad, he was there so she could hand him the supplies they'd brought along with them and offer her a hand out of the helicopter once everything was unloaded. He shielded her from the wash of the props as the helicopter took off again, all but disappearing into the night sky, except for the flashing green and red light that identified the craft.

"How was dinner?" Toneau asked as he began to pick up their supplies from the deck where she and Tuck had stacked everything.

"Really good. Doctor Dupré's aunt is an excellent chef."

"Glad you made it back, Cap. We got the cannon brought up from the site as ordered."

The news was like an electrical shock of excitement—a combination of Christmas, birthday, and New Year's expectations all rolled into one. She clutched her hands together and bounced up to the balls of her feet. "Where is it?"

Toneau nodded toward the stern. "Down in the lab on the conservation deck, prepped and waiting for you. We've had it in a plain water tank for the last three hours to help begin desalinization, and Guereaux has already photographed it for you."

She thrust her packages into Toneau's already laden arms and dashed off the helipad to the stairs to the decks below, taking the steps two at a time. There wasn't a moment to waste. The second an artifact was brought up, especially a metal one exposed to the corrosive salts in seawater, the clock to stabilize it and prevent damage started ticking. True to his word, Rory Guereaux was already there.

"Doctor Dupré, glad you're back. Isn't she exquisite?" He gestured toward the cannon.

In all honesty, it looked like a crusty gray, oddly shaped log with a rough surface and misshapen rounded bits, but he was correct—even in that state it was a thing of beauty.

"I've already taken measurements and recorded it photographically."

"By the look of it, you haven't started cleaning off any of the larger encrustations."

"I thought you'd want to see it first."

She nodded. "Your instincts are absolutely right." She walked around the cannon looking it over, absorbing the details for her notes. It was on the small side for a cannon at less than three feet long. Two small rounded hubs on either side of the back of the cannon, which would have rested in the fork, helped her identify it. It was the *peterero*, or swivel gun, mounted in a fork on the upper deck so it had more movement and a broader range. "Has the electrolytic solution been prepped?"

He smiled. "Added the sodium carbonate myself, and the anodes are ready to go when you are."

She preferred the sodium carbonate method to sodium hydroxide, especially on a moving ship where the alkaline solution could harm someone if it wasn't handled properly. By running a current through the water, they'd neutralize the corrosion of the metal happening from the exposure to salt water. Metal objects were always a crapshoot as far as Bella was concerned. If the desalinization process happened too slowly, you could end up with something so fragile it would simply fall apart into rusty flakes. If you did it too fast, well, then you had a whole other set of problems.

She made sure the stainless steel anodes were set in the right place on the electrolysis tank and the end wires prepped to attach to the cannon, then flipped the switch to turn the electric current on, and let the solution sit while she gently and carefully removed some of the larger buildups of material on the cannon that would slow the whole process down. Using small hammers and wooden picks, they tapped off some of the larger bits of foreign material that had accumulated over the centuries, and used wire brushes to get to the metal. She and Guereaux worked quickly, his large hands moving just as deliberately and sure as her own.

"How soon do you think we'll be able to determine if this is from the *Rapid*?" he asked while he worked.

"Depends on if the foundry stamp is still legible or if we can make out other identifying markers. Could take a few days, might take a week or more. It all depends how thick the encrustation is on the cannon and how long it takes to neutralize it and clean it up."

They worked together for a long while, the radio playing county music in the background, until the cannon was ready to be submerged into the electrolysis tank. They put on gloves, goggles, and rubberized lab aprons to protect themselves from the solution, and Guereaux carefully hooked up the hoist to the cannon, using straps designed not to mar it, but still sturdy enough to bear the weight.

Slowly it lifted, swaying slightly as the hoist stopped over the tank, then began its descent. Little bubbles rose up from the surface as it was submerged.

Bella slipped the goggles back over her head. "A good night's work, Mr. Guereaux."

"It's Rory. No need for the formality if we're going to be working side-by-side in the lab for hours on end."

She smiled. He was right. Once they started bringing up

other artifacts, this lab would be home for the duration of her trip. She'd hardly see Tuck, except perhaps at meals. She thought about The Kiss, and decided that would probably be a good thing. "Okay, Rory it is."

"If you'd like to look at the photos and archive information, it'll be on the main computer system. You should be able to access the data from your laptop or from the computers on board."

She smiled. Having someone assist who actually knew what they were doing when it came to proper preservation technique was unexpected and welcome. She'd been dreading having to keep the crew from being ham-fisted with the finds and potentially damaging them with beginner's mistakes. "Well, Rory, you're not just a pretty face. You know your stuff, I'll give you that. Where'd you study?"

He smiled at the compliment. "Master's in Maritime Studies from East Carolina University."

She nodded. "It's good to have someone I can trust in the lab."

"You didn't think I'd leave you to do all the brainiac work alone, did you?"

She turned at the sound of Tuck's voice. He stood in the door to the lab with his arms crossed, which showed off the muscles of his arms to their best advantage. "I'd had my suspicions," she said.

He nodded toward the cannon. "Happy?"

She couldn't stop the smile that stretched from ear to ear. "Deliriously happy! In a day or two, hopefully, we'll be able to confirm if it came from the *Rapid*."

"So that means you have some free time at the moment?" he asked, a teasing grin making her instantly recall exactly what his lips had done to her earlier, and how much she'd been anticipating it happening again. Her skin tightened in response. She glanced back at Rory. "You'll turn out the lights and make sure the lab is locked?"

He waved her off. "Go on. If I can't babysit a big iron cannon, then I'm not much use."

She stepped out of the lab past Tuck. As soon as they were out of sight of the lab, she felt the weight of his hands on her hips, pulling her back and into the warm, solid heat of his body.

"So what did you decide? Have you changed your mind about short-term relationships?" he said softly in her ear, his breath caressing her neck and making her shiver.

Her pulse picked up. What had she decided? The tattoo had to be a sign, didn't it? Why else would she have dreamed of it? And while she had no illusions about Tuck staying for anything other than the short term while they worked together, should that completely keep her from enjoying herself? *Make a decision, girl.*

"How about you follow me, and I'll *show* you my answer."

Chapter Nine

Tucker was hoping with every fiber of his being that Bella intended to tell him yes, she had changed her mind. Even better would be if she said that what they'd started outside her aunt's house in the French Quarter was only the beginning.

She held his hand lightly, her fingers entwined in his as they went single file down the narrow corridors of the ship, past the polished teak paneling and doors with gleaming brass handles to where both his and her berths were located. Bella put her hand on the doorknob to her cabin.

"Do you mind if we go to mine instead?" he asked.

She turned, eyeing him. "Any particular reason?"

He hesitated. What he wanted to say was the bed was bigger, but until he knew for certain that was what she wanted, he decided it would be smarter to keep that to himself. "Bigger cabin?"

Bella nodded, giving him a teasing grin. "Why is it always about size with you guys? Fine. Your room then."

He went ahead one door down and opened the door for her. As she passed by him into the room her fresh scent of citrus and sugar teased him, making his mouth water and his dick hard. He'd tasted it on her skin in the darkened alley and craved more. In all honesty, waiting for her to finish her preliminary work with the cannon and keeping himself out of the conservation lab for several hours had been torture. His brain was fixated on remembering the feeling of her beneath his hands, the smooth texture of her skin along the waistline of her shorts, and the soft, supple feel of her mouth. Damn, he wanted more. Now. But that wasn't up to him.

He shut the door behind them, his whole focus sharpening, zeroing in on her. It was the thousand little details about her that etched into his brain: the small, damp curls of wispy dark hair against her neck, the way the shade of her lips changed from darker pink at the edges to a paler pink where they were fullest, the way the second button on her shirt strained a bit as she sat on the edge of his bed and leaned back on her hands. He thought about popping all those buttons off with his teeth, one by one, then helping himself to what lay beneath.

He crossed his arms, first to keep himself from just spreading her out on the bed, and second because he wanted her to know she was in control. He wouldn't make a move until she asked him to. Not this time.

"So dinner at your aunt's house was…eye-opening," he said, trying to give her the opening to decide which way the conversation and the evening ahead of them would roll.

Bella's sexy full lips twitched. "Is that what you'd call it? Frankly, I was way more interested in what happened after we left, weren't you?"

Oh, hell yeah. His temperature spiked up a notch. His fingers itched to touch her, but it was still not a green light.

"Which part was your favorite?"

She stood up from the bed and walked over to him, her eyes sultry, lids lowered in a come-get-me look that made his dick throb. She stepped closer, her smooth index finger touching his lips. "Everything from here," she said, caressing his bottom lip and then slowly moving it down his chin and throat, her hand sliding down his chest and stomach until she hit the bulge in his pants and cupped him firmly, "to here."

He groaned at the sensation. *Green light, go.*

Tuck scooped her up in his arms pulling her into him. There was no preamble to the searing kiss, no tentative buildup. When Bella unleashed herself, she was an unexpected firestorm. He hadn't realized how much she'd been holding back or that it would take his breath away.

They pulled off clothing as quickly as they could, still kissing, until she was left in just her bra and panties. Pulling off his shorts and ripping off his shirt had taken him a fraction of the time she'd spent unbuttoning her shirt. She wrapped her arms around his neck, and with a hop wrapped her long, silky legs around his waist, her hot, damp panties pressed against his raging hard-on. He ground against the heat. Bella let her head fall back, deep sounds of pleasure resonating from within her. "Yes. More of that," she said, her voice husky as she rolled her hips, pressing against him.

"Whatever the lady wants." Her boldness freed him to return the favor. He kissed down the silky length of her neck, enjoying the sugar and spice that cloaked her skin. His hands kneaded over her supple body, the round, firm curves of her ass fitting perfectly in his palms. With his fingers he pulled aside her panties, letting the hard length of him slide against the slick, wet heat she offered and tried hard not to let go. She bucked, rubbing herself against him until she panted and arched. His knees shook.

"Please tell me somewhere in this room you have a condom."

He laughed and carried her to the bed, every muscle shaking with need. God, if there was an award for restraint, he'd fucking earned it. "One condom coming right up."

He pulled out a packet from the dresser, and Bella snatched it from his hand, ripped it open, and grabbed hold of him, sliding the condom over him as she licked a path down his stomach. His breath hissed between his teeth. Baseball. Football. Hell, he'd think about soccer. Just hold it together. Let her set the pace, even if it killed him.

The heated scent of her was driving him wild, but the sight of her skin sheened with sweat, eyes fevered with desire, and the touch of her hand pulling him forward and into her blew his world apart. There was no holding back. Her fingernails raked his skin, and Bella cried out, panting.

They collapsed on the bed together, both sweating and breathing hard like they'd finished a marathon. "Worth waiting for?" he asked as he traced the curve of her cheek and smoothed back the damp curls around the edges of her face.

"Oh, yeah. Definitely." She smiled and deep down something in his chest hitched making it hard to breathe. Bella wasn't exquisite; she was extraordinary.

For all his flirtations, he wasn't one to bed an endless stream of women like some of his college buddies. They said his standards were too high for something he never intended to keep. He liked to think he was being selective, but nothing had prepared him for Belladonna Dupré in all her naked, wanton glory.

She rolled, putting her arm over his stomach and laying her cheek against his chest, her body soft and languid against his. For a moment everything felt right in the world. For a moment he was content.

A knock at the door woke them.

Toneau's voice sounded muffled through the door. "Captain, we've found a debris field."

Bella had never seen a man move so fast in all her life. Tucker launched out of the bed and yanked on a pair of shorts before opening the door a crack. She appreciated the fact that he blocked the view of the crewman on the other side of the door.

"I'll be there in two minutes," he said, then shut the door and turned to face her. "Can you be ready—"

She beat him to the question and was already buttoning her shirt over her bra.

The corner of his mouth tilted into a grin. "I like a woman who can dress, and undress, at the speed of light. It's a handy skill."

She swept her hair up into a crazy bun on her head and threw an elastic band around it to hold it in place. She cocked her hip to one side and gave him a sassy look. "I've got lots of hidden skills you've yet to discover."

"Let's test that theory." He moved across the room, gathering her up in his arms, and lifted her off the floor. Bella wrapped her bare legs around his waist, and he kissed her like he hadn't seen her in days, his fingers trailing down her spine and cupping her bottom.

Bella broke off their kiss, breathing hard. He was ready to go and so was she, but he'd put a deadline on them. "You told Toneau two minutes. That was four minutes ago. We'd better go."

He released her enough to slide down the length of him, and her body was all too aware of the perfect hard-on he had ready to go as she swept down and over it. Deep at the V of her legs her body contracted and pulsed.

"This isn't over." He cupped his hand around the base of her head and kissed her thoroughly.

"I'll hold you to that." Bella yanked on a pair of shorts, practically pointless since her panties were soaking wet, but then the crew didn't need to see her in her underwear.

They headed down the hall, and Tuck held out his hand toward the stairs. "Ladies first."

"You're only saying that so you can look at my ass as we go up the stairs."

He grinned. "You know me so well."

Just to tease him she put an extra swing to her hips as she climbed the stairs and heard him growl behind her. Their affair might be short-lived, but what it had in intensity sure as hell made up for duration. She'd savor every moment and store them up.

They'd made love again three more times during the night, and each time Tuck had shot her to the stars and back, making her feel both well-pleasured and adored, then let her fall asleep against him. She hadn't felt so safe, so loved in a long time. *It's an illusion*, she reminded herself. *Enjoy it while it lasts.*

She and Tuck crowded into the bridge with the other eager crew to look at the ROV findings. The images the transponders had help capture showed clearly the outline of a debris bed that look like it extended for several hundred feet, as if an object had been dragged across the sea floor littering it as it went.

"Look at the glass!" Bella pointed to the bottles, scattered hodgepodge in the deep sediment, but clearly visible and many still intact. "That has to be a merchant ship."

"Don't get your hopes up," Tuck said. "It may not be the *Rapid*."

"Even if it isn't, it's still a hell of a find," Williams said, excitement in his voice as he pulled on the length of his beard.

"Is the ROV ready to start removing sediment so we can really see what we've got here?" Tuck asked.

"Aye, cap. We've also got it fitted with the basket already," Toneau said.

Tuck grinned. "Then what are we waiting for? Daylight's

burning. Let's get some things up here for Doc to look at." He pulled her close, hugging her to his side.

Deep down the fluttery sensation in her stomach told her this had to be the *Rapid*. Excitement and expectation bubbled through her veins like fine champagne. Life couldn't get any better that this.

F or the next five days, the ROV trolled the debris field using the six-inch diameter Venturi hose to vacuum sediment off the finds and filter them into compartmentalized baskets attached to the back of it.

One after another the baskets came up, full to the brim with dozens of small items, buttons and grape shot, coins and spoons. Each larger artifact was carefully lifted with the ROV's flexible rubber limpets and placed in a numbered recovery basket, its position systematically documented by Barclay, Scott, Williams, and Reeves who logged data and kept the machines moving. Each of the recovery baskets was sealed into protected multiplex units for their voyage to the surface, and Bella stood in awe as they began to stack up.

She and Guereaux were working for as long as they could each day, photographing and documenting each piece before they received first-aid conservation and were stabilized enough to be put into temporary storage for transportation to her lab at Fontanel & Company where the bulk of the restoration would happen over the next few years. There was simply too much to be able to do a full restoration on each piece.

The good news was the stamping on the cannon confirmed it *was* from the *Rapid*. The bad news was, it made Bella all the more anxious. Where was the hull? Where was the crystal ball?

On the afternoon of day six, the phone in the lab rang. Bella pulled off her gloves and wiped the beads of perspiration from her forehead with the back of her hand. She felt like she hadn't seen the sun or Tuck in days, even though they shared their meals together every night, sometimes with the crew and sometimes without, and always slept in each other's arms.

"Conservation lab, this is the doc," she answered.

"You're going to want to come up to the bridge to see this," Tuck said. The energy in his voice pulsated through the phone line.

"I'm really slammed, are you—"

"Bella, get up here. We've found the *Rapid*!"

Bella dropped everything. "Rory, they found it! They found it!" She hugged him around the neck and sprinted out of the lab, taking the stairs on all three levels two at a time so she could reach the bridge faster.

There on the screen in glorious color, like watching one of the Jacques Cousteau documentaries she'd seen as a kid on the Discovery Channel was the hulk of a ship, blackened ribs arching gracefully over the hull of remains. Barclay maneuvered the ROV slowly, recording all of it.

Bella inhaled with awe and delight. "Look! You can see the copper sheeting that wrapped the base of it," she said, bouncing up on her toes. "I can't believe it! We found it, we actually found it!" She spun around and grabbed Tuck in a fierce hug and kissed him hard on the mouth, not giving a damn if the crew knew or not. It was a moment to celebrate, and she could think of no one else she'd want to share it with than him.

Toneau called down to the kitchen for champagne, and Williams broke out a store of cigars he'd been saving for such an occasion.

Tuck went to help get glasses, and Toneau followed. Toneau pulled him aside in the corridor. "Cap, you know I'm not one to pry into your personal business, but what are you and the doc up to?"

"I thought you said you aren't one to pry."

Toneau shook his head. "I know, but something's changed between you and her. Everyone can see it in the way she looks at you and the way you two touch one another when you think no one's looking. Problem is on a ship this size someone is always looking. And that kiss wasn't just a kiss of excitement over finding the ship."

"What if the doc and I have an understanding? How's that anyone's business?"

"It ain't. Not exactly, except you got us all under a no-fraternization rule. We look up to you for that, and a man can't lead what he don't follow."

Tuck ignored the twist in his stomach. Deep down he knew sleeping with Bella was asking for trouble, but they'd both gone into it knowing this was only for the short term— no promises, no expectations. So what was the harm in that? Sure, she'd like it to be more, she'd made that clear, but she knew not to expect it. The problem was she deserved more. Hell, she deserved better than him. She deserved a man who would put her up on a pedestal and believe she was the greatest thing that had ever happened to him, and he just wasn't that guy. He couldn't be, not if he wanted to rectify his past and be more than the man his father was.

"You want me to talk to the crew?"

Toneau smirked. "That'd be one hell of a meeting." He shook his head. "No, word will get around quick enough if you let key people know that you and the doc have decided to be an item. It's the hiding it that they won't understand. Feels like you're telling them to do one thing but not following it yourself. Now if you change the rules we all go by, then fine, no harm."

Tuck nodded and put his hand on Toneau's shoulder. "You're a good man."

The problem was, Tuck thought morosely, was *he* a good man?

Now that they'd found the wreck, the countdown clock on his relationship had started ticking. And while he admired Bella and had never met anyone like her, the tendrils of a romantic relationship were still too binding for his taste. Oh, he was tempted. Hell, yeah he was tempted, but years of seeing what being in an uncertain relationship had done to his mother still kept him latched on to the one thing he knew to be true. In the long-term, relationships that hooked into your heart and kept you tethered were ones that destroyed you, no matter how in love you thought you might be.

Chapter Ten

"You need to take a break." Tuck stood at the entrance to the conservation lab, his arms crossed, tanned torso bare, looking terribly…distracting. It took a moment for her brain to reengage and actually process what he said, instead of staring at him and enjoying the view.

The sound of Rory opening a multiplex container to bring out another basket of items recovered from the *Rapid* snapped her out of her daze. Within a day of positively identifying the cannon, they had started working the site, and the amount they brought up was staggering. Days had started to blend together as she worked sixteen-hour shifts. "Do you see all these containers? How on earth can I take a break? Half of this isn't even photographed or cataloged yet."

He sighed and shook his head at her overdramatic tone. "You need to get out of this lab for a little bit. You and Rory have been working non-stop for a month. If you don't get some sun and a little R&R soon, you're gonna snap."

"I am not!" She looked over at Rory. "I'm fine. We're fine, aren't we?"

Rory refused to make eye contact with her and shook his head, too. "I'm not the boss, Doc. If the captain thinks you need a break, he's probably right."

Tuck stepped into the lab, getting close enough she could almost taste the sea spray on his skin. "All work and no play makes Bella—"

She stopped him with a finger on his lips. "There's plenty of play, and you know it," she said low enough for only him to hear.

The corner of his mouth lifted in a sexy, knowing smile, and he kissed her finger. "Doesn't mean you don't need to get out of here for a break."

"Like what?"

"Come dive with me."

"Dive?" She wasn't sure she remembered how. During one of her courses she'd been required to try it a few times, but not enough to become certified in it or to do it as a sport. Basically, she'd learned the science behind it, gotten wet a few times, and left it at that.

"You've snorkeled, right?"

She nodded. Snorkeling was easier. Simple. Minimal commitment. Bella frowned. Maybe she had as many issues with commitment as Tuck did. But then she'd never met a man she could rely on before to not eventually hurt her somehow.

"Same difference. Use your mouthpiece, only big thing is you keep breathing with it instead of going to the surface, and you always dive with a buddy. How'd you get out of knowing how to dive if you were studying underwater archeology?"

"I studied maritime archeology and history and rely on big, burly guys like you to do the grunt work and bring everything to the surface," she replied.

"Grunt work. You greatly underestimate my value, Doctor Dupré."

She glanced down at the broad expanse of his bronzed

chest and the muscles covered with taunt skin. Tuck could have been a work of art. She traced down his chest with her finger, enjoying the ripple and flex of his muscles in response to her touch. "Oh, I don't underestimate," she said with just a hint of seduction. "I like to mess with you."

The blue in his eyes grew bright with arousal. "You can't properly call yourself a scientist in underwater archeology until you've at least been on a dive. Take off your lab apron, and get in a swimsuit. I've got Toneau prepping our equipment now." A sexy, slow smile spread across his lips. He nodded his head and raised his eyebrows twice in a quick bump. "We're going down."

It felt like he was issuing her a challenge. Fine. She'd accept. She'd snorkeled dozens of times and had gone diving a couple of times. How hard could it be?

"You're on." She untied her lab apron and set it aside. "You going to be okay on your own for an afternoon, Rory?"

"He'll be fine," Tuck answered. "Right, Rory?"

"No problem, Cap."

Tuck winked at him, and Bella wedged past him and headed toward her cabin to change.

A half hour later she was on deck, stuffed into a neoprene wetsuit, a weight belt, a buoyancy compensator vest with tanks strapped to her, fins, a mask and snorkel, and a regulator all in place. "I didn't remember there was so much extra equipment," she muttered.

"Don't worry. You'll do fine." Tuck had been giving her a quick, mini-diving class, explaining all the equipment and adjusting it to fit her properly. Every time his hand had brushed her bare skin, she had to repress a shiver of yearning for him to strip it all off her and carry her back to his cabin.

An afternoon spent in bed seemed like a lot better form of rest and relaxation to her than diving, but Tuck assured her it would be an experience she'd never forget. All her diving until now had been in the deep end of a pool or shallow lake. Three dives in all, and only to pass a required class.

"I'm going in first, so I'll be in the water in case you need anything. Remember foot out, step off, hold your mask, keep breathing," Tuck said.

Bella nodded then watched his every move as he stepped effortlessly out over the water and splashed down, bobbing back up to the surface.

"Go for it, Bella!"

She pressed her mask to her face with one hand and clamped her lips around the hard plastic of the regulator as she lifted one finned foot out over the edge of the boat over open water and stepped out. The cool water hit her in a rush. She kicked up twice and bobbed up to the surface, making sure to tip her head back so her wet hair wouldn't obscure her mask.

The first big difference she noticed was the gentle ebb and swell of the ocean waves. That hadn't been a factor in either the pool or the lake. The current wasn't too strong, but she could feel the gentle tug and pull of it as the water moved around her. He made the diver signal for okay, and she responded back with the same signal then motioned for ready to dive. She double-checked her regulator, breathing in. The familiar Darth Vader-like sound assured her everything was working fine, and she plunged beneath the waves.

Sunlight streamed down in white and gold ribbons from above, constantly rippling like they were in a breeze as the pale blue of the water surrounded her. It seemed endless, stretching out in all directions simultaneously. The bright yellow bottom of the *Discovery* bobbed on the surface, her only connection to the world above. Tuck was already swimming away. She let her arms float back to her sides and kicked hard, letting her fins do the work as she followed him down.

Exhilaration had bumped up her heart rate, which would mean a shorter dive if she sucked up the air in her tank too quickly. Consciously, Bella slowed down her breathing. She wanted to extract every minute she could out of the dive with Tuck.

She pulled in a deeper breath than she intended. All along these past few weeks she'd been savoring every moment with him, always the ticking clock in the back of her mind knowing that no matter how good they were together, the end was coming faster and faster like a bullet train. Emotionally, she was tied to the damn train tracks and going to get run over if she didn't keep at least part of her heart to herself. But for now, in this moment, it was all worth it.

The sense of freedom was amazing, like being a fish herself. For a moment she let her neutral buoyancy allow her to hover in the water and the gentle sway of the current rock her. It was so damn relaxing. She could understand why he loved it so much. It fit him. And he fit her. And who knew, maybe fate was fickle enough to let it all work out. How, she had no idea. That was still a mystery. She kicked off again, trailing behind Tuck.

Spadefish, flat and thin like giant black and silver striped angelfish, meandered in a glinting cloud in the water, some of them chasing after the bubbles that rose from them in a trail as they dove deeper. They seemed serene, until something changed. An instant later the school moved in perfect synchronization as they darted and disappeared to avoid perceived threats in the water.

She heard their threat before she saw it, the clicks and high-pitched whistles of a pod of dolphins streaking through the water above them. Their supple, smooth bodies undulated as they swam, sometimes brushing against one another, other times breaking the surface. Bella tugged on Tucker's BC vest and pointed up at the dolphins. He winked at her and gave her a thumbs-up. This was probably the coolest thing she'd done in years, definitely the kind of stuff that made a guy date-worthy. So was this a date? In a twisted kind of way, she supposed it was. After all, it was just the two of them in this watery wonderland.

It was hard to tell which direction they were swimming down here without a sun in the sky to guide her to east and west. There was only light up above and dark down below. She knew the area they were in was deep, but not as deep as it could have been. They were on a shelf of sorts, where the wreck had landed, but the deep water was close by.

The farther down they went the darker it grew. Less light could penetrate from the surface, and she swam close enough to Tuck to make sure she could reach out and touch him at all times.

Tucker flicked on his flashlight and tapped her arm, pointing to the light clipped to her BC vest. She unhooked it and flipped her light on, too. The beam cut through the darkness, and she could see more sea life, corals, some thin and fragile like leafless bushes, others shorter and thick, like tentacles from an octopus, a few feather-like, seemed to sprout from the mix of sand and stony outcroppings at the bottom of the ocean. Colorful sea stars, orange, red, and purple of different shapes and sizes, and a variety of fish meandered through the coral, on a search for food. It was beautiful, like being in the tank of tropical fish rather than just looking at it.

Tuck grasped her hand, his fingers interlacing with hers. He squeezed her hand, and her heart swelled. Being down here like this with him made her feel as though it were only the two of them in the world. Together they swam, hand in hand, using their fins alone to propel them slowly over the alien landscape. Tuck squeezed her hand twice and pointed at a small red octopus moving through the coral. She nodded, and he swam closer to it to investigate. Personally, she had no interest in getting up close with something that squishy.

Tuck moved the beam of his light so that the edge of the halo lit up the octopus, but it moved quickly, too quickly, and into the brilliant center beam of the flashlight. It jetted upward in a red streak and almost collided with her as it darted past her and into the dark water beyond.

Bella sucked in a startled breath only to find water entering her mouth instead of air. While her instinct was to cough, she fought it, spitting the water out instead and trying desperately to hold on to the air she had left in her burning lungs. She waved frantically at Tuck, but he was turned away and didn't see her. She kicked quickly until he was within reach then rapped hard on his tank.

He spun around, eyes growing wide behind his mask the minute he saw her lift up her faulty regulator and her panicked motions at her throat. He yanked his regulator from his mouth, blowing out a slow stream of steady bubbles as he handed it to her and reached for the back-up regulator he carried on his tank. Blessed air flooded her lungs as she inhaled.

He motioned to the surface, and she nodded. There was nothing more they could do down here now. They would have to both use his tank on their way to the surface. Halfway up they stopped for a decompression break, and Tuck checked the gauge to see just how much air they had left. He frowned, and then motioned upward.

Both of them knew if they didn't stay long enough at this depth to decompress, they risked getting the flood of expanded gas bubbles in their bloodstream that divers called the bends. But since they were sharing the air that was left in his tank, getting back to the surface was a top priority, even if it meant they had to wait it out in the recompression chamber afterward.

They moved toward the light, but not fast enough. Bella took a drag of air off his regulator and instead of getting lungful, got only a sip. Tuck registered her panic and pulled her with him as he lunged toward the surface. They broke through the surface. Bella gasped as they hit the air and for a second floated, her head leaning back on her BC vest so she could suck in great gulps of air. She was lightheaded, and her body ached.

"Fire up the chamber!" Tuck yelled at the crew as he pulled her over to the metal ladder that hung down over the edge of the ship into the water. Her muscles were trembling, her skin itching, and she was so dizzy she could barely stay upright. Tuck put a hand at her lower back to help her as she climbed up. She thought Tuck was no better, but he kept making sure she was okay.

"Keep going, Bella. We've got to get into the recompression chamber ASAP." Not easy to do when her legs felt as reliable and wobbly as soft-set gelatin.

The minute she sprawled out on the deck, Toneau and Barclay started stripping gear off her and Tucker, pulling the heavy tanks and BC vests from their backs and helping them up.

She tried and fumbled with the zipper to her wetsuit.

Tuck grabbed her hand. "Don't worry about it. I've got it." He quickly and efficiently peeled her out of the wet neoprene, his hands cold as they skimmed her flesh, and then pulled off his suit as well.

Both of them were given towels, dry clothes, and bottles of water before they were placed in the cylindrical recompression chamber. It was stark white inside, with one fold down bunk against one wall and a series of fold-down chairs along the other. Clear and black tubing hung suspended from the arched metal ceiling and connected to face masks with elastic on them like those found in airplanes.

The door clunked into place. "Are you feeling dizzy still?" Tuck asked. He pulled down the fold-away bed from the wall and yanked back the blue utility blanket and white sheet and placed a towel down for her.

She nodded and swayed a bit as she sat down on the bed, her ears popping as the pressure in the room increased. "Put your mask on and lie down," he said. After about ten minutes of breathing the oxygen, the fuzziness in her brain receded.

"What happened?" Her words were muffled by the mask.

Tuck sat next to her and shrugged. "We came up too fast."

"Never had the bends before."

"That's good." His words were muffled, too, his nose and mouth covered, but she could see his eyes. Those cool, clear blue eyes that made her feel relaxed. Even after just ten minutes on the oxygen, she felt better.

"So we're stuck in here?"

"For the time being." A gleam in his eye told her exactly the direction his thoughts had taken. "This is going to work out better than I expected," he said.

"Better than you expected? We're stuck in a decompression tank while we could be bringing up and cataloging things from the *Rapid*."

"Well, yeah. The upside is, the crew will keep that part going. And usually you're stuck in here by yourself, or with another guy. But," he said, as he hung a towel over the view portal of the chamber, "being forced to be alone, in here, with you for hours, when we've got nothing but a bunk, now that's hardly an inconvenience. More like a perfect opportunity."

"How are you feeling?"

"Better."

He pulled off his oxygen mask and hers, and curled up beside her on the bed, wrapping her in his arms. "You're cold. If we huddle together, we'll warm up faster."

As she ran her fingers gingerly across the shadow of stubble on his chin, and along the smooth edge of his mouth, he exhaled and kissed her fingertips, and Bella realized how delicate the balance of life was.

Tuck had sacrificed his air supply to ensure they both made it to the surface. He'd saved her. Deep within her, the last innermost wall she'd kept around her heart crumbled. Those weren't the actions of a man who'd leave you to fend for yourself with a broken heart. He'd done something for her no other man in her life had ever done—he'd risked his very life for her. If that wasn't love, even without the words, she didn't know what was. She knew one thing for certain— she could trust Tuck. He'd do anything for her, including risk himself. And that changed everything.

"I think we'd both warm up considerably faster if we got out of our wet swimsuits," she said.

"Doctor's orders?"

She could feel a slow, sassy smile lift up the edge of her mouth and nodded. He took her hands in his and pulled her up from the damp towel she'd been lying on.

"Then we shouldn't waste any time. I'd hate for you to catch a cold on my watch because I didn't follow the doctor's instructions." He yanked off his swim trunks in one fluid motion, and they landed on the floor with a wet slap. He looked down and kissed her, his mouth warm and hungry against hers as his hands trailed around her ribs, then slipped around her back. His clever fingers quickly untied the strings of her bikini top at her back and her neck, and it fell away. The heat of his hand against her breast replaced the cool air that brushed over her now bare skin. He cupped it, cradling it in the palm of his hand as the broad pad of this thumb teased the tip, turning it hard despite the warmth he offered her. Bella groaned as his tongue matched the stroking sensation of his fingers, while the silky, hot length of his penis pressed against her belly. Slick heat spread between her folds in response.

"You've done great so far, but I think you can do better," she said. At her waist, the fingers of his other hand flexed, kneading her skin, then slipped loose the bikini ties at her hips, slipping the scrap of wet cloth away from her. Despite being naked against him, she wasn't cold any longer. Her skin was flushed, and the sensation of his bare body against hers was more than enough to warm them both.

"Anything else?" he teased. Bella lifted up on her toes and arched against him, and he responded to her demand. Then his hand lowered, the heel of his palm pressing against her mons in slow circles as his fingers slid through the damp seam and dipped inside, teasing her. She opened herself to him, wrapping one leg over his hip, rubbing herself against the hard shaft, but keeping herself at enough of an angle that he didn't enter her.

He shuddered. "No fair," he said.

"Who said I play fair?" she whispered back. She pulled away from him for a moment, then touched herself with the palm of her hand and fingers until she was wet with her own juices. She grabbed hold of his hard length with her wet hands, and he flexed at her touch and let out a slow hiss of breath between his teeth. She stroked the silk over steel. Tuck closed his eyes, his head falling back.

"You know there'll be payback." His penis jumped again in her hand, throbbing in response to her, and she gave a throaty laugh.

"I'm counting on it."

Tuck lowered himself, bringing his face even with her belly, then bent lower, his rough cheek brushing against the tender backside of her knees as his hands cupped her bottom and kneaded. His hot kisses trailed upward higher and higher along the inside of her thigh, making her stomach quiver and her head light. Bella leaned back against the bunk for stability. Her knees were growing far too wobbly to hold her up all by themselves.

He placed his hands behind her knees and pulled forward, forcing her to rest her weight on him. Tuck lifted her until her back lay flat on the bunk and her thighs were splayed across his shoulders. He lightly nipped the inside of her tender thigh.

"Hey!"

He gave her a wicked grin. "Payback."

"You won't win," she said, her voice husky.

He lifted one dark brow, his blue eyes almost getting lost as the pupils dilated and grew bigger. "Watch me."

He kissed and nibbled at the most tender parts of her, driving her mad, making her squirm as the need for release coiled tighter and tighter within her. She almost came undone the instant his warm slick tongue slid between her swollen folds and expertly flicked the little nub. He caressed her with his hands, undid her with his mouth until her head thrashed, her damp hair sticking to her cheek.

"Uncle," she said, between pants.

"What?"

"Uncle. You win. You've proven your point. Now, before I fall apart, I want to feel you inside me."

He rose, his body glistening with sweat, every muscle rigid as if he were about to explode and held it all together through sheer force of will. He pulled her up from the bunk and lifted her, pressing himself fully into her. Bella cried out in pleasure and wrapped her legs around his hips and her arms around his neck for support. He kissed her deeply, even as he moved within her, and the rhythm increased, propelling them to the edge of the abyss. Bella tangled her fingers in his hair, desperate to hold on as the tension within her spun out of control. Never had she felt a release this fully, body, mind, and soul entwined with a man.

She shattered in his arms, and he followed her. They lay

together on the bunk, their bodies slick with sweat and glued together, his heavy form atop her, both of them breathing hard in the humid heat of the chamber. It took a moment for the rounded room to come back into focus, and for that moment, Bella relaxed in how blissful it all felt.

"I think we can both count that as a win," she said.

She felt him smile against her skin. "Good. Next time you get to determine who challenges first."

"Next time? I'm boneless here."

He chuckled. "And we've got another four hours left. We can get at least another two rounds in." He lifted up on his arm and looked at her, his blue eyes deep and languid like hidden deep water in the bayou. "How about the best two out of three wins?"

He kissed her lightly, nibbling at her lips, and when his fingers stroked leisurely down the length of her bare back, the touch did more than just arouse her, it went deeper, making her feel desired, precious—loved. Tuck didn't treat her like some fragile thing to be placed upon a shelf; he treated her like a flesh and blood woman with real wants and needs. And right now she wanted him, all of him.

Chapter Eleven

Five hours later, after barely coming up for air, they were both starving.

No one had disturbed them in the recompression chamber. It had been a mini-vacation of sorts, just the two of them, though not at all the kind of vacation Bella would have preferred. She'd imagined some place tropical, with sugar-white sand and aquamarine water, rather than the institutional nature of their current accommodations. But it had been good. In between making love, she'd finally gotten a chance to just lie beside Tuck and talk with him. She thought she had a much better insight into him now and what it would be like to live with a man like this. *Don't bet on it, girl. Just because he saved you, doesn't mean he's staying.*

Bella shoved aside the nagging doubts. "What do you want to do when we're done with the salvage?"

"Go to New York." Face deadpan, eyes sharp and hard, he seemed to withdraw. Not physically, he still held her, but emotionally Bella could feel that he'd already gone.

Her chest ached. "Okay, not what I would have picked."

"And what would you pick for me?" he asked, tracing his finger down the indent of her spine, sending spirals of heat washing through her. He kissed along the route his finger had taken, and she shifted, rolling over in his arms. His mouth came down warm and possessive on hers.

"Maybe you setting up a dive shop or fishing boat for tourists out in Key West or Jamaica or having a sailing-tour operation."

He smiled. "Hmm, that does sound way better than New York."

"What's in New York?"

"Unfinished business." He pulled back, sitting up on the narrow bunk they shared. The sudden absence of his touch and the sour edge of his tone made Bella think twice about pressing him for more information. She suspected it had to do with the McCormacks—a topic best left alone for both of them.

"But after that, then what?"

"I was hoping you'd tell me," he teased.

"Well, we could start off by doing more of this." She ran her hand across his chest, letting it drift down across his abs to the crisp line of hair just under his naval and stroked him with her fingertips.

"Good call." His lips curled into a predatory smile. "Does that mean you'll go diving again with me sometime?"

"I'm not diving again."

A sad look entered his eyes. "Look, I know this time was bad, and I blame myself."

"Why?"

"I should have double-checked your equipment myself. Made sure you'd be safe."

Bella shook her head. "Accidents happen."

His gaze was sharp. "Not on my watch." Even after he'd ensured they'd made it back safely, that he'd literally sacrificed his own air to breathe to keep her alive, he still blamed himself.

Bella realized Tuck was like a fish out of water stuck on dry land. He needed to be near water, thrived on it, and if she refused to go into the water ever again, it would create a barrier between them she couldn't bridge. So she stuffed her fears down and tried a compromise perhaps they could both live with.

"How about I meet you halfway and we snorkel instead?"

A brilliant smile lit up his face, and he kissed her on the forehead. "Yes. Absolutely."

Bella questioned just how much of herself she was willing to give up to be with him. He'd risked his very life to be with her. Was she willing, or even able, to do the same?

The intercom unit on the wall crackled. "Ready to get out of the tin can?" Toneau asked.

Tuck leaned over and pushed the com button. "I thought it would take longer."

Toneau laughed. "Thought or hoped?"

"Both."

"Well, the doctor we've been in communications with did the calculations. He wants us to run a blood test on you both to see if enough of the nitrogen has migrated out of your blood stream, and if it's good, you're free."

Bella quickly threw off the blanket covering them and pulled on her clothes. Tuck did the same as the big wheel on the front of the chamber rumbled as they spun it to open the hatch door.

Toneau popped his head inside the chamber. "How's the happy couple faring?"

"Ready to be released into the wild," Tuck answered as he gestured for Bella to go first.

How were they faring? Tuck didn't really know. Things had changed between them, big time. He'd done what he'd had to in order to get them back to the surface safely, but having Bella at risk had made him crazy. Worse, it made him think about his world without her in it.

As much as he wanted to be with her, he could feel the tendrils of attachment curling and constricting around him. He'd fallen for her, there was no doubt about that, but he didn't dare call it love. Love meant pain, and Bella was anything but pain. She was more like air, as necessary to him as his next breath, and yet, if he got too used to relying on her, he'd never finish what he'd started. He'd never be his own man—able to look his half brother in the eye and let him know, you didn't destroy me, and now it's time for payback.

He needed that closure to feel free of his past. It was the one thing he still hadn't talked to Bella about, the deepest, darkest part of him that wanted revenge. It was an ugly thing. Tuck didn't like that part of himself, but he acknowledged he owed a debt to it. That dark desire had driven him to greatness, pushed him to succeed when everyone else said things were impossible.

All he needed was one more big score to have the money to strip Phillip "Dickhead" McCormack of everything he valued and send him for a little strength-of-character training of his own. It was one thing to be born with money and to have always had it. It was another to be brought up like a prince of Wall Street, then have yourself stripped down to the bones and rebuild. Phillip had no idea the shit storm that was coming his way.

Now that they were out of the chamber, Tuck felt pressure to get as much up from the wreck as they could. They'd already brought up a lot, more than some salvages, as the contents of the wreck hadn't been picked over. But it wasn't enough. He wanted the big score—that diamond "crystal" ball the size of his fist—if it actually existed.

Despite everything they'd brought to the surface that was the golden ring, the goal that pushed him harder. Bella wanted it, and he'd damn well get it for her. He wanted her to see him as a guy worthy of waiting for. He wanted to build a life with her—after he'd taken care of cleaning out the crap his family had left him. Once he did that, he'd be ready for anything.

Problem was he didn't know for certain how long it would take. They'd have to process, preserve, and sell off enough of the treasure for him to see a substantial profit. He needed several million more beyond what he'd already amassed to be able to buy out the McCormack Group flat-out. That could take time. Deep down he believed he wasn't capable of a serious relationship until he could excise the demons from his past, and he wasn't sure Bella would understand the wait.

For another two weeks the whole crew worked hard. They were quickly running out of multiplex containers and needed more. Bella was thrilled with the haul they'd brought up so far, but the niggling doubt that the crystal ball hadn't been found still bothered her, like a bug bite that needed to be scratched. Nothing was going to be good enough until she scratched that itch and found it, because while she didn't believe in the Dupré family curse, she wasn't willing to cast it off altogether as fable. And whatever she had going with Tuck, she didn't want to jinx it.

Evening was falling, and the sky was streaked with brilliant slashes of red and vibrant orange as they stood together on the deck of the *Discovery* watching the sunset. "Red sky at night, sailor's delight," Tuck said as he held her close, his arm around her, his hand resting comfortably on her hip.

"The perfect end to a perfect day."

"No, the beginning of a perfect night," he said, then brushed a kiss on her neck. "Come for a night swim with me."

She couldn't see how snorkeling or diving at night would be any fun. The water was dark, and there wouldn't be much to see, but it was warm and balmy, and a soft breeze ruffled over the water. "I'll go get changed into my suit."

"Need any help with that?"

She winked at him. "I think I can manage."

Ten minutes later they were in the water. He'd convinced her to put on snorkeling gear and bring along a flashlight, even though she felt silly for doing so.

"I don't understand why we can't just go swimming," she said as she treaded water and the ocean current rocked her back and forth. As her hands moved and the fins on her feet stirred the water, it filled with the brilliant blue sparkles. "Oh! That's beautiful! Look at the bioluminescence."

He smiled, his teeth white in the dark. "There's more to see in the dark than you think, Doc." He pulled his mask up from around his neck and into place. "Ready?"

She nodded, and they put their snorkels in place and swam out away from the lights of the ship. Bella glanced back and saw the trail of blue light behind them. Tuck snapped on his flashlight and put his head in the water. She followed his lead. Ahead of them in the dark water a sea turtle, his wide-finned legs cutting through the water, seemed to float like a hovercraft in the endless ocean. Minutes later a school of fish, startled by their light, pooled together in a giant writhing ball that moved and flashed in their light beams like a giant living disco ball.

Just as her legs were growing tired and weak, they dipped under the water and swam back in the direction of the ship. Ahead of them was enormous translucent jellyfish, which looked like a ghost the size of the loveseat at the house, pulsating in the water. Long, thread-like tendrils moved like fringe on a flapper dress as it danced through the sea and disappeared into the dark.

They both popped out of the water, and she motioned back to the ship. She reached the ladder first and climbed up, slipping off her mask and fins and slicking back her wet hair out of her face. She watched, waiting for Tuck. He left a trail of bioluminescence as his fins churned the water, leaving a glittering blue trail of quickly fading light behind him as he rose like a god of the sea.

He climbed up the ladder, shaking the water from his hair, his teeth white in the moonlight as he smiled at her. The temperature of the air was slightly cooler than the water, chilling the exposed skin of her legs faster than the rest of her. Bella pulled against her wetsuit, but the tight-fitting neoprene didn't want to budge.

"Here, let me help you with that."

Droplets of seawater sparkled on her skin in moonlight. Even the tips of her long lashes, nearly black in the night, were tipped in glistening transparent beads of light, making her look as if she were dusted with diamonds.

"You remind me of a mermaid."

"How's that?"

"Just watching you move in the water. You're beautiful, alluring, enticing, I'd even say a little bit bewitching."

She laughed, the sound throaty, soft and sweet—a lover's laugh. "And what will you do now that you've caught me, sailor?"

"I believe it's traditional for you to grant me a wish," he said as he shucked off his neoprene suit and let it join hers on the deck.

"Don't tell me; let me guess." She rose up on her toes and wrapped her arms around his neck and kissed him hard, pressing herself against him. Hell, now she was a mind reader, too? He wasn't about to complain.

He swept her up into his arms and carried her to the stairs that led down to the cabin level. How they made it down the stairs when neither of them were looking where they were going because they were too busy kissing was anyone's guess. Frankly, he didn't care. He just wanted to get Bella back into bed.

He'd never met a woman that he shared such sexual chemistry with before. The way she moved, the small noises she made as she came undone in his arms all drove him over the edge every time. And even when they were curled together in sleep sometimes, she'd nudge the amazing curve of her ass up against him in her sleep, and he'd get hard all over again, and she'd be wet and ready to go.

They made it to his cabin and got inside. "Bed?" he said as they still devoured one another with kisses.

"Shower."

"Shower?"

"Seawater makes me feel sticky."

"Sticky doesn't sound so bad," he said, but then a shower didn't sound so bad, either.

He turned on the water in the shower, letting it run until it was warm and the room filled with steam, then pulled her in under the hot spray. Her skin pebbled and her nipples turned hard at the temperature change. But he'd fix that. "Need a little help?"

The hot water was heavenly, but having a naked Tucker in the shower made the temperature irrelevant. Everything he did, the way his hands slid against her skin and his mouth closed around the rigid peaks of her breasts spun her up. He suckled, shooting threads of pleasure down her body to the very core of her.

"Now that you're warm, how about a little soap?" He grabbed the bottle of body wash and poured a measure of it into his hands, rubbing them together to form suds. "Turn," he instructed. Bella knew better than to question. He seemed to know what she'd enjoy without her saying a word.

He brought his slippery hands around her waist, tracing her ribs and cupping her breasts, as he rubbed the lather all over her. Next he trailed down, across the flair of her hips and over her bottom, kneading and rubbing her slick flesh against the hard muscles of his thighs and abs. His erection slipped between her thighs and slid against her lips, making her quiver with need. She knew precisely how good he'd feel. She lifted on her toes, changing the angle enough to have him slide deep inside her. Bella gasped.

He moved, holding her hips in his hands, his clever mouth kissing her neck as he set a rhythm that made her dizzy as her breath came in short, quick gasps. Sparks shot through her vision, like the glowing blue bits of bioluminescence in the sea. She felt her world blow apart, then come back together, and still he held her in his arms.

He turned her, tucking her in close against him. The spray had lost its heat and was growing colder. "I think you need a towel." He opened the shower door and grabbed a towel, gently rubbing her down and kneeling as he did so, kissing down the length of her body, her collarbone, her breast, her stomach, thighs, and behind her right knee.

They left the bathroom and tumbled into bed. Bella was sure her bones had melted. She relaxed into him as they curled together.

"Bella?"

"Hmm."

"I have something I need to tell you."

She rose up on her elbow and looked at him. "My hair is a disaster?"

He glanced at it, a smile tugging at his lips. "No, your hair is beautiful. You," he paused to kiss her, "are beautiful."

"You either have low standards or are very nearsighted," she said.

"Neither."

"What did you need to tell me?"

He shifted position, and she could sense the uneasiness in him. Immediately she thought it was something about his family, or worse still that it had been fun, but that it was time for them to move on.

"Do you remember how you were adamant about knowing who was funding the operation?"

She nodded. "I needed to know what kind of people I'd be sharing the find with. There have been a fair share of partners who run off with the money in these kinds of endeavors."

"I have a confession. I'm your partner."

She giggled. "I should hope so, otherwise I'm in bed with the wrong man."

He took her hand in his, massaging his thumb in small circles against her palm. "No, I'm serious. I funded the salvage."

Bella frowned. It didn't make any sense. She knew he'd said he didn't need the money, that the acknowledgment was more important, but all of this, the *Discovery*, the helicopter, the crew, all belonged to *him*?

"Why didn't you tell me?"

"I just did."

"Why didn't you tell me *sooner*?"

"At first, I didn't want you looking at me like I was an endless bank account."

"Why would I do that?"

"Most women do."

"If you haven't figured it out already, I'm not like most women."

"Agreed." Tuck kissed the back of her hand. "I wanted to be sure we were partners in this. I didn't want you feeling like my money should give me more say in the operation of this ship than I already had as captain. You were so worried about the *Rapid* that I didn't want to make you any more uncomfortable than I already was."

"You still should have told me sooner."

"Did you trust me?"

"No. Not at first."

He lifted her chin with the crook of his finger looking deeply in her eyes. "I didn't trust you at first, either, but I sure as hell found you attractive."

"And now?"

"Now I'd trust you with anything."

He held her close, the stubble of his chin against her temple softer now that it had grown out a few days. Bella lay, her leg across his hip, her body curled against his and his arms cradling her. It felt not just good, it felt right, perfect even, if there was such a thing. Bliss. That was a better word. She closed her eyes and inhaled the unique blend of sun, sea salt, and man that was Tucker. "I love you," she said as she exhaled.

He tenderly brushed his hand over her hair and kissed her forehead. "You mean the world to me."

It wasn't I love you, but Bella would take it anyway. Tuck had proven himself to her in so many different ways, looking out for her, protecting her, sharing his secrets with her. Perhaps, given his childhood, it was something he didn't ever say. She let contentment wash over her as they fell asleep in each other's arms.

In the middle of the night, Bella woke to the soft sound of Tuck breathing in and out next to her. The waves beat in a languid rhythm against the hull of the ship, a soothing sound that should have helped her fall back to sleep. But it didn't.

She hadn't told Tuck about her suspicions, although she'd debated about it. Hell, what was there to tell him? She didn't even know for certain herself. All she knew was that her period was late. It wasn't as if there was a corner drugstore aboard the *Discovery* to go get a pregnancy test. She needed to know for certain before she said anything to him. If it were a glitch from too much stress, or too much physical labor, telling him and then rescinding the claim would only alienate him. She was sure of that.

No. Until she took a test, she wasn't going to say a word.

Chapter Twelve

Bella stood with her arms crossed looking at the wall of full multiplex boxes she and Rory had constructed with the help of the crew as items had come up from the *Rapid*. The large plastic totes took up one whole wall in the conservation lab. "You see what I mean," she said to Tuck, gesturing to the boxes. "Our holding area is almost full. We need to take some of this back to Fontanel & Company."

He nodded. "I'll have some of it shipped back and call a helicopter to come get you and some of the more fragile pieces."

"It'll be a quick trip. I'll make sure they're logged in at the company and be back by dinner." After almost three months aboard the ship with only one or two breaks, Bella was ready to head ashore. As much as she appreciated and liked Tuck's crew, and Tuck, there was just too much testosterone on board.

Then there was the pregnancy test. Until she got back ashore, she was still playing a guessing game. She needed to know, and, if it was positive, then he'd need to know.

Two hours later, the helicopter was loaded and ready to leave. Another ship had been called out to load up the multiplex totes and ferry them back to Fontanel & Company, but it would take it another hour to get there and three hours to get back to New Orleans. That meant that once they touched down, she'd have the afternoon to take care of her personal affairs before seeing to the logging of the crates.

"You should stop by and see your aunt," Tuck said. "I'm sure she misses you."

Bella smiled. Exactly what she'd had in mind. "Good idea. I'll do that."

The minute the helicopter touched down, Bella started the clock ticking in her head. She had only a few hours to get everything done she needed to. She'd called ahead, and lab assistants from Fontanel & Company met them to help unload the more fragile items that had come with her.

Once those items were secure, she took her car that was parked at the docks and drove to the drugstore, grabbed a test and the biggest bottle of water she could find, and made a beeline for her aunt's shop. If anyone could help her make sense of all the jumbled-up mishmash of feelings and thoughts in her head, it was Aunt Min.

The wind chimes over the door made a familiar tinkling sound as she entered the shop. Aunt Min was talking with a customer, deep in a discussion about some ink from the sketch paper she had spread out on the countertop.

Min made eye contact with her, smiled, and gave a nod of greeting. Bella knew she'd get to her when she could. In the meantime, she headed for the back room where the stairs up to Min's office, the employee bathroom, and kitchen area were located.

She'd managed to drink three quarters of the bottle of water on the way over. Considering it was a pee test, she wanted to make sure she had plenty of answers. Bella hurried into the bathroom and pulled out the package, the scientist in her slowing down long enough to read all the directions twice, then took the test, and set a timer on her phone. All there was left to do was wait.

A knock sounded on the bathroom door. "Bella, you okay, *cher*?"

"Yeah, just needed the bathroom. I'll be right out." *In five minutes.*

Four minutes later Min knocked again. "You sure you're okay?"

No. She was not. Bella opened the bathroom door, and the minute her aunt saw her face, she was enveloped in a big hug. "Bella, what's wrong?"

She glanced at the pregnancy test sitting on the tank of the toilet. Aunt Min followed her gaze, and then her eyes got wide. "Are you?"

She nodded, because she was still a little too surprised to speak. Sure she'd missed her period, but deep down she hadn't believed it until she'd taken the test. Now there was no denying it. She'd have to tell Tuck.

Min hugged her again, this time even harder, then pulled back, and with a mother's touch tucked a strand of hair back behind Bella's ear. "Who's the father?"

Bella tipped her head to one side and pricked up a brow. "I'll give you one guess, and Jackson Palmer doesn't count."

Min pulled her over to a chair in the connecting kitchenette. Her eyes narrowed. "Does he know?"

Bella shrugged. "How could he? I found out a minute before you did."

"Well?"

"Well what?"

Min rolled her hand. "Do you think he'll be happy about it?"

"Knowing Tucker, no. He's not the white picket fence type of guy. And his childhood was messed up enough. He probably has a phobia about being a father."

"But he's been good to you?"

Bella grabbed hold of her aunt's hand. "Yes. God, yes. He's an amazing guy. And we didn't plan for this to happen, any of this."

"But you couldn't fight it, either," Min said.

Bella blushed.

"He's that good, huh?" Min teased. "Kind of thought he might be. When are you going to tell him?"

"When I get back, the moment I get back."

"And what if he doesn't want it?"

Bella pulled back her shoulders and took a deep breath. "Then I'll figure it out."

Downstairs the chimes sounded as someone entered the shop. "I've got to go downstairs. You take as much time as you need. There are chamomile and peppermint teas up in the cupboard."

Her aunt hurried downstairs. You had to love Aunt Min. She was a free spirit, willing to go wherever the wind blew her. For her it was always an adventure. Bella put her hand on the flat of her stomach. Hard to believe soon she'd be a mom. Not that she'd hadn't thought about it before. It was just that without her own mom or her *grand-mère* around, she wasn't sure who to ask the questions she'd need answers for. Bella shook her head, her hand falling away from her stomach.

If worse came to worst, she'd raise her child in her family home. There was more than enough treasure from the wreck to pay off what they owed and set them up nicely for years to come. Hell, if she really wanted to, she could quit her job at Fontanel & Company and stay home to raise the baby herself.

So it didn't matter what Tuck thought. Either he'd want the baby or he wouldn't, and no matter which it was, she'd sink down roots here in the city and raise her baby in the same place generations of the Dupré family had.

After she and Aunt Min had shared dinner over some of the most divine chicken and rice she'd tasted in ages, she took the helicopter back to the *Discovery*.

There were lights and music and even some of the crew dancing, drunkenly, of course, but still dancing. Tucker helped her out of the helicopter, a million-watt smile on his face.

"Boy, do I have news for you!"

Likewise, Bella thought.

"We found it! This afternoon, we did some additional excavation and found the remains of a safe of sorts."

Dread turned to a fizzing of excitement. "You found it? Did you find the crystal ball?"

He picked her up by the waist and swung her around and laughed. "Yes! We found it! It's beautiful. Do you want to see it?"

She beat a fist on his shoulder. "Of course I want to see it! Are you going to put me down or carry me there?"

He chuckled and let her slide down the length of him, then kissed her. It was warm and full of happiness and excitement. For a moment she could have almost believed the curse was broken, but then she hadn't told him her news yet. Bella didn't want to spoil his mood.

"Come on, this way!" He grabbed her hand and pulled her along at a jog to the conference room where a tub of water sat on the table on top of a towel. At first it looked like there was nothing in the water, but Tuck put his hand in, and as he lifted it, the curve of the crystal ball rose above the surface, gleaming and sparkling in the overhead lights.

Far from being a perfectly smooth sphere as she'd thought

it would be, it was an orb created from a thousand different facets. It looked round, but it glittered and threw rainbows all around the room. She sucked in an awed breath. Whoever had crafted it had to have skills far beyond their time. It was exquisite.

Tuck held the orb out to her. "This, Bella, is for you."

She stretched out her hands, and he let the weight of it fall into her palms. It was heavier than she'd imagined, a true piece of stone. While very clear, she could see minute inclusions in the stone as she turned it in the light. She wouldn't know until she looked at it under a microscope for sure. She breathed on it, and when it didn't fog, like quartz would with warm breath, she knew the fairy tale was real. There was a good chance it was a diamond.

"It's incredible!"

"Are you happy?"

She grinned at him. "Deliriously happy."

"Good. Then mission accomplished." He kissed her on the mouth, and the crew made catcalls and wolf whistles. For the second time that day Bella blushed. If they only knew.

Bella gingerly placed the orb back in the water container. Whether it was diamond or not, there was sure to be salt residue on it after being in the sea for so long. She turned to Tuck and placed her hands on his chest, as he pulled her into him, his arms around her waist.

"Any chance we can take this party somewhere more private?" she asked, her voice low enough the others wouldn't hear.

His grin got wider if that were even possible. "Sure." He grabbed her hand and led her up the teak stairs to the lounge area where they'd danced what seemed like a lifetime ago.

She went to the railing and leaned on it, looking at the clouds coming in that were playing hide-and-seek with the moon. Tuck came up beside her, his shoulder and arm brushing hers.

"So were you surprised?" he asked.

"Absolutely."

"Why don't we order up some champagne? We just found a legendary lost item."

She dropped her head, staring at the waves churning around the boat. "I'd better not."

"Afraid I'll take advantage of you?" Then his tone changed. "You don't seem very excited about this. Is something wrong, Bella? Are you worried about me leaving when this is all done?"

She locked gazes with him. There was no time left. She had to tell him. "I'm pregnant."

"**H**ow?" She speared him with an incredulous look. "Really? Do I have to explain it to you?"

Tuck ran his fingers through his hair, making the already awkward angles even more disarrayed. "No. I mean, I get it. It's just that we used protection almost every time. This wasn't supposed to happen."

Bella nodded. "There's a reason they don't say 100 percent effective as a marketing slogan. They can't."

The thought of a baby was horrifying and short-circuited his brain. A baby? That was the ultimate tie, the one that couldn't be broken.

He often wondered if his mother had deliberately gotten pregnant with him to ensure that, as the mistress, she wouldn't lose her hold on his father. Just the thought of being a family man twisted him up inside. The problem was he didn't know how to be one. His own upbringing did absolutely nothing to prepare him for raising another human being.

It also brought into question his relationship with Bella.

In a nanosecond it had gone from a fun fling to something he couldn't walk away from even if he wanted to. There was only one thing he knew for certain right now—he wouldn't walk away. Even if he was a lousy father, at least he'd be present in his kid's life and provide for both him and his mother.

His heart contracted painfully in his chest. What if Bella didn't want to be with him? What if she'd already accepted that they were something short term or that she wanted someone who could be a homebody, which wasn't him? Could he handle letting some other guy raise his kid? No. Wasn't an option. Bella would be stuck with him, regardless. Hell, they'd both be stuck with each other.

She waved her hand in front of his face. "Earth to Tuck. Come in, Tuck."

He blinked a few times and stared at her. "Sorry. What?"

"Sometimes condoms fail."

"Yeah. I think we've established that."

She nibbled at her bottom lip, worry clouding the clear green of her eyes. "So now what?"

"I guess we have a baby," he said simply.

"There are other opt—"

"No. There aren't. If you're pregnant, I'm taking care of you and my kid. End of story. I'm not going to be an absent father like I had. Not now, not ever."

Bella nodded, her hand grasping and holding on to his forearm. "Thank you, Tuck."

"For what? Finding your crystal ball or getting you pregnant?"

"For sticking by me instead of running for the hills."

Tuck pulled her close and kissed her. "If anyone was going to have my baby, I'd want it to be you. I'm not saying this will be easy, but it's doable. Look, if we can find a treasure that's been hidden for over a hundred years in the middle of some vast piece of ocean, we can raise a kid together."

He noticed the dark smudges below her eyes. "Let's get

you into bed."

She grinned. "Are you always going to say that?"

"As long as you'll let me."

Tuck woke to find the captain's berth filled with the rosy glow of sunrise. He glanced down at Bella still asleep beside him, her dark hair cascading in silky waves across her pillow and down the glorious smooth skin of her naked back.

As tempted as he was to spoon up against her soft body and go back to sleep, he knew he needed to get his day going. He slipped out of the bed, careful not to wake her, pulled on a pair of shorts and a tank top, and headed up to the bridge.

Toneau was there already, a steaming cup cradled in his big hands. A second mug for Tuck sat waiting for him. He wasn't sure how, but Toneau always seemed to know when he was coming and had straight-up dark coffee waiting for him.

"Red sky at morning, sailors take warning," Toneau said, repeating the nautical nursery rhyme and taking a sip of coffee.

"No shit." Tuck picked up his mug, the warmth of it seeping into his hands, and looked out at the thickening bank of clouds painted hues of red, orange, and gold by the sunrise. Beautiful, yes, but a bad omen. Those clouds were the front edge of a tropical storm system headed in from the southeast toward the Gulf. Williams had been tracking it through the night.

"What's the word from NOAA and NHC?"

"Tropical Storm Henri turned hurricane about five hours ago. Now up to a category two. Tracking right now to pass south of Cuba and head up the coast of Mexico."

Good for them. Not so good for Mexico. With any luck they would just catch the edge of it, and their dive work would only have to take a brief hiatus.

"How far out is it?"

Toneau shrugged. "Anywhere from six to twelve hours depending on how strong it gets."

Tuck wasn't willing to take the chance it might change course and rob them of their find. "Get everyone up and moving. I want the wreck tagged with GPS transponders and floats in the next four hours. That way even if it moves in the storm surge, we'll know where it went."

"Still kind of risky, Cap."

"But a calculated risk. That's something I can work with." Tuck took a sip of his black coffee letting the bitter, burnt taste of it wake him up. "I'm not losing the *Rapid* when we've only just found her."

After making the necessary arrangements, Tuck headed back down below with a cup of coffee with cream and shot of vanilla syrup for Bella and a second cup of straight-up coffee for himself. He opened the door to his berth quietly. Bella was still curled up asleep in the tangled sheets.

"Time to rise, sweetheart."

She mumbled something unintelligible, snuffled a bit then rolled over, pulling a pillow over her head. He grinned. Bella was not a morning person. Normally a great thing, since it gave him ample opportunity to enjoy her being in his bed before he had to get up. But today it wasn't an option.

"Bella, you need to wake up. We're having an all-hands meeting in the conference room in half an hour." He set her coffee down on the nightstand, and she shifted slightly beneath the sheets toward the scent.

"Half an hour," the mumbled words came from under the pillow. "That's not even time for me to get my eyes open."

He pulled the pillow off her head and grasped the edge of the sheet. "Well, open or not, dressed or not, you need to be at the meeting in half an hour." He slowly pulled at the sheet and Bella fisted her hands around it in a death grip.

"I'm getting up. Don't make me cold as well."

He chuckled. "Your coffee is on the nightstand."

"Thank you," she said.

"Don't make me come get you."

She muttered a few choice words and sat up, brushing the tangle of hair back with her fingers. The sheet dropped to her waist, exposing the rosy tips of her breasts. He resisted the urge to tackle her back to the mattress and feast on those fabulous breasts.

He swallowed hard. "I'd wear more than the sheet."

She chucked the other pillow on the bed at him, and it hit the door with a soft thud as he left the cabin.

Half an hour later Bella showed up to the conference room, looking practically perfect. Her glossy dark hair was scooped up into a ponytail that skimmed the tops of her shoulder blades, and her freshly washed face looked soft, her lashes still dark with moisture. She had a glow about her that could only be described as radiant.

He held his breath for a second, trying to slow down the sudden kick in his chest and instant pressure in his groin. He'd seen her naked in bed. Why the hell did seeing her in a tank top and cut-off jean shorts seem just as erotic? He could get addicted to this, to seeing her every morning.

Tuck tore his gaze off of her and cleared his throat, making an effort to look anywhere in the room besides at her.

"As some of you know, we've been tracking the movements of Tropical Storm Henri. As of six hours ago, it strengthened into a hurricane and is headed for the south edge of the Gulf."

"Why don't we head back to port?" Bella asked. A few members of the crew nodded in agreement.

"First, there's not enough time for us to tag the wreck and make it back to port. Second, you don't want to be in port when a hurricane hits. Last thing we need is a vessel torn up and stranded on land." Some of the experienced crew mumbled agreements under their breath and glanced at one another.

"You're telling me it's safer out here in open water? I think the crew of the *Rapid* would beg to differ. Don't hurricanes sink ships?" Bella asked.

He had to look at her, to focus on her, and get her to understand. This wasn't his first storm and, luck willing, wouldn't be his last. "Trust me. We'd do better out here, especially if it tracks on the predicted course and runs south of here and into Mexico."

Toneau spoke up as well. "What about nonessential crew? You want me to call out the helicopter and get them evacuated? We could get them back to shore before the storm rolls in."

He knew Toneau was thinking of Bella, but there were at least four to six other crew that didn't need to be there to ride out the storm. He doubted Bella would go willingly, but she might go with a group. "Yeah, get them on the phone and arrange pickups."

"Aye, Cap." Toneau slugged down the last of his coffee, got up, and headed for the bridge.

"How far out is the storm?" Andre asked.

"Williams, you want to fill us in?" There was no point in relaying information that could come directly from the source. Williams had been monitoring the situation closely all night.

"The storm is anywhere from four to ten hours out from us and moving fast. Right now it's hovering between a category two and three but getting stronger. Tracking to just south of Cuba and scheduled to make landfall on the gulf coast of Mexico in about twelve hours."

Tuck took over. "We need to get the ship ready for the storm, and we'll be sending down the ROV to tag the wreck with floats and a transponder. That way we'll have a better chance of locating it if the storm surge moves it. "

"Isn't that cutting things a bit close?" Bella asked.

"All the better reason to get moving. You have a half hour to get the ROV, floats, and transponder ready to go. I want this wrapped up in less than two hours."

She waited until the rest of the crew had left before she approached him. "Just an FYI—I'm not leaving to go back to shore."

He'd suspected she'd resist. "There's nothing you can do out here while we ride out the storm. You might as well take some of the artifacts we've already uncovered back with you and begin working on them in your own facilities."

"You're trying to get rid of me."

He put his hands on her arms. "No, I'm trying to protect my ship, our project, this crew, you, and our unborn child, and right now you putting up another road block isn't helping."

"You don't understand! We have to catalog these finds. Without that, they're practically worthless! You won't be able to prove their provenance without them."

"No, *you* don't understand. We've got a hurricane coming. A goddamn hurricane! And none of this will matter if we lose it all."

She frowned. "Fine, but I'm not leaving without some of the artifacts that are too fragile to handle being bumped about in a storm."

Yourself and our child included, he added silently. The diving incident had shown him stark reality that Bella was not a water baby. Yes, she could swim, but out here, if she wasn't one with the water and something happened to the ship, she'd die. That simple. And he wasn't willing to take the risk. She meant too much to him.

"Go pack what you're taking, and have Rory get it prepped to load in the helicopter when it gets here."

Bella turned on the heel of her bare foot and headed down to the conservation deck.

The next half hour was a blur. Men rushed to get the

ROV ready to go, even as the chop in the water began to increase and the surface of the sea was whipped up into white caps. The clouds overhead had lost their rosy glow and instead were thick gray wool pulled over the sky, making the air humid and hot.

Sweat trickled down his temples as he worked alongside his crew. They angled the magnetic end of the boom in place and lifted the ROV into the water. The minute it splashed down, Tuck checked his watch. An hour and a half and counting.

He was serious about the two-hour timeline. They needed to ensure the ROV was back on deck and secure before the front edge of the storm hit. He glanced at the sky once more. Pale gray was giving way to hues of dark gray and purple, the dark color of eggplant. Not good.

"Captain, we've hit fifty feet," Barclay reported on Tuck's earpiece.

"What's the condition?"

"Good amount of surge in the water in the top fifty feet. Had a hard time compensating and had to turn on the reserve thrusters to get the ROV to go where we needed it, but it's better now. You can definitely tell the ocean knows something is coming," Barclay said.

"Get it down to the *Rapid*, get the transponder set and activated. If you can't place the floats and get back here in under the two-hour limit for the dive, then don't. I want that ROV back on deck and secured in an hour forty-five."

"Aye, Captain."

Tuck clicked off the earpiece and went looking for Bella. His earpiece buzzed again. "Yes?"

"Helicopter is on its way out. Should be here in an hour," Toneau said.

Good. At least something was going to plan. "Make sure that Doctor Dupré and any of the artifacts she's taking with her are on it."

Chapter Thirteen

An hour later Bella found herself lifted off her feet, put into the helicopter, and strapped to a seat. Rain pelted down, needle sharp, and the wind ripped at her clothing. Several other crewmembers from the *Discovery* were already on board.

"I told you, I don't want to go!" she shouted over the roar of the helicopter engine, the wash of the prop blades, and the incoming storm.

The hard planes of Tuck's face and the ice-cold certainty in his eyes told her he wasn't budging and was furious. Rain plastered his hair to his head and dripped off his determined chin. "Staying is not an option!"

"But the rest of the artifacts, we need—"

"We don't need to do anything! You're going ashore. You can't just think of yourself anymore. This is what's best for all of us."

Bella placed a protective hand over her still-flat stomach as his words hit home. He was right. She was being stupid and selfish, risking her life and the baby's, just to stay onboard with him. But dammit, she didn't want to go. Not without him.

She grabbed his arm, her fingers digging in. "Come with me." She hated that she sounded like she was begging, but in the moment it didn't matter. A flash of memory, her gripping her father's sleeve, begging him not to go when she was five, pierced her brain, making her face and torso turn hot and her eyes burn. Deep down, something was telling her that if she and Tuck were separated, it would be final. This would be the end, and she'd never see him again. "Come with me," she said again, still waiting for him to reply.

Tuck frowned, his jaw flexing, and he closed his eyes, pain etching his features into a distorted mask of fury and agony. "You know I can't. I have to stay here. My crew needs me."

"I need you," she almost sobbed. "Our baby needs you. You told me you'd stay."

His eyes snapped open, the blue now blazing, like the hottest part of a flame. "Don't do this to me, Bella. Don't make me choose. I'll contact you as soon as everything is taken care of and all clear."

She choked back the thick, hot feeling in her throat and let her hand slip from his skin. "I love you."

Cupping her face, his thumb brushed against her cheek with such tenderness it nearly broke her heart. He nodded and kissed her, his lips firm and yet soft on hers, letting the depth of his emotion come through in the kiss when words failed him. She understood. He was both telling her he felt the same and good-bye.

He glanced at the pilot and gave a single curt nod, then pulled back and shut the door. Inside, Bella thought she might burst. Hot tears welled up at her eyes, and her fingers trailed along the rain-spattered glass as the helicopter lifted off the deck of the *Discovery* and into the darkening sky.

Sometimes he felt as if the universe were conspiring against him. People always said if fate handed you lemons, make lemonade. But what happened when it handed you shit?

Fists clenched, Tucker strode back to the bridge. When Toneau handed him a towel, he muttered, "Thanks," and roughly wiped himself down. A lost cause. His clothes were still wet from the increasing rain outside.

The chop was getting worse and the ship beginning to sway. He hated sending her away like that, but what the hell else was he supposed to do? He couldn't leave, and she couldn't stay. That was that. End of story.

"Cap," Williams's grim tone caught his attention, "hurricane has changed course. It's growing stronger and tracking northward."

Right into them.

Fuck.

Would you like another helping of shit? No, thank you. But it got handed to him anyway.

"Is the ROV secured?" He'd barely had time to check on it while he made sure Bella and what artifacts the helicopter could accommodate were packed on board.

"Aye, Cap," Barclay answered. "Secure. Transponder and floats placed on the wreck are good to go."

"Good work." He glanced at Toneau. "Get us the hell out of the direct path of the storm, and keep tabs on that transponder."

"Aye." Toneau's normally carefree demeanor was gone. They were down to a skeleton crew, just five of the team left on the ship, and they were still loaded with cargo brought up from the *Rapid*.

If they made it out of this, it would be a major coup.

The whole time she'd been sitting on the helicopter, all she'd been thinking of was Tuck. Her only consolation was that she'd brought the crystal ball back with her. If there was a curse on her family, it would end with her and Tuck. Fate could go screw herself.

The crew from the *Discovery* took care of transporting the cargo into the Fontanel & Company truck. There was only one box she was worried about, and she took that one in the car with her as she drove home.

The streets of New Orleans were deserted and smelled of water on pavement. Water slewed down the streets in little rivers over the cobblestones as storm drains maxed out. Shops were boarded up with hasty pieces of cheap plywood. Wind whipped the palm, crape myrtle, and oak trees and blew debris around as the power of the storm increased. At least she'd had the foresight to call ahead while she was on the helicopter and let Aunt Min know she was coming.

She made it back to the French Quarter as the sky grew even darker. Rain was coming down harder, lashing against the car furiously enough that the windshield wipers on full could barely keep up. The only blessing was, in this weather she wouldn't have to fight the tourists for a parking spot and could park right outside the house. She grabbed the plastic tub from the passenger's seat and ran inside, shoving the door closed hard against the increasing wind that grew stronger as it tunneled down the narrow streets between the old brick buildings.

"Are you dripping on my floor?" Aunt Min called out in welcome as the door slammed shut.

"Got a towel?"

"Right there next to the door, *cher*."

Bella set the plastic bin down and hastily dried off. Between the artifacts inside and the liquid they were stored in for preservation, it was damned heavy. "I'm going upstairs to change," she called out. She took the plastic container up to her adjoining bathroom and set it down in the tub, so that if anything sloshed out it wouldn't be on her bed or the floor.

Before she did anything else, she wanted to reassure herself that the crystal ball was safe.

Bella quickly dug through the rest of the pieces, desperate to find the orb. There'd been four identical boxes, with the most precious of the artifacts stacked side-by-side, and she'd grabbed the top two, which was all she could manage.

But the crystal ball wasn't there.

"It's the wrong box!" The crystal ball was still on the ship with Tucker.

Bella staggered into her bedroom and collapsed onto her bed, her knees suddenly too weak to hold her upright. Deep in her chest an ache bloomed, spreading outward like a dark oil slick on water. She curled up, bringing her knees to her chest and wrapped her arms around her legs.

Fate was a cold-hearted bitch. If that crystal ball was still out there with Tuck, then odds were the *Discovery* was about to become another shipwreck.

She watched the storm coverage on television until the power went out. Aunt Min lit candles and brought her a blanket and rubbed her hand in soothing circles on Bella's back, but the dark, cold feeling invading her bones couldn't be soothed that way. What if he died as so many other men over the centuries who'd dared to love a Dupré woman had?

"He's going to be fine, Bella. It's just a hurricane. We've been through worse."

Bella nodded. Her aunt said the words, but her eyes mirrored the worry lodged in her own chest. There was every chance Tucker and the ship might not survive.

"Do you want some soup?"

Bella shook her head. Hell, she wasn't even able to summon one-word answers anymore. She refused to believe in fate. Refused to believe that she'd lose him, and that took every ounce of energy she had left.

Min frowned. "Maybe you ought to sleep."

Sleep. Yes. And just let it all fade to black. Bella lay down on the bed, the blanket tucked around her, and listened to the wind howling outside and the clatter of a loose shutter somewhere in the house as it banged against the sturdy bricks of her family home.

Stay safe, Tuck. Stay safe. Come back for me.

For the next four hours, the remaining crew of the *Discovery* put all their energy in fighting for their survival. Clouds, dark purple, gray, and black, swirled overhead, bringing a torrent of rain, as if the sky poured a giant bucket over them.

The storm lashed out, tearing away bits of the ship in the high winds and sloshing them about as the *Discovery* roller coastered on black waves sixty-feet tall. The sea crashed over them, scouring away everything on deck that wasn't secured. The ship moaned and creaked in protest at the beating it received. Just staying upright was a challenge. Every muscle he had ached with the effort of holding on.

Eventually the storm moved on to bigger and better destruction, no longer interested in toying with them. The sea slowly leveled out, but the sky stayed dark. Night had fallen while the storm raged. Only flashes of lightning in the distance on the back edge of the storm could still be seen on the dark horizon.

They sat in the conference room, every one of them physically, emotionally, and mentally exhausted, but alive. And that was something to celebrate. They cracked open a few bottles of beer. As far as he was concerned, every man on board more than earned his cut of the treasure. Even though there was more to bring up, what they had already found was more than enough to make them all very wealthy. But it had never been about the money, not for him. Going through the storm had brought things into sharp focus for him. Making a name for himself with the discovery of the *Rapid* wasn't enough. He couldn't start a life with Bella until he freed himself from his past. Having a baby only put a ticking clock on how quickly he needed to sever ties. And to do that, he needed to confront his half brother Phillip and take control, ultimately tear apart, and sell off the McCormack Group. He wouldn't be the victim of his genetic ties any longer.

It was another three hours before they could get their communications gear up and running again. Everyone was exhausted. They were sixty miles away from the wreck and the transponder they'd pinned on it had stopped working. Best-case scenario—the storm hadn't moved the wreck, and they could get back to work. Worst-case scenario—the wreck had been moved by the storm, and they'd have to work at finding it all over again.

Right now he had to be content knowing Bella was safe, his ship and crew had survived the storm, and he had unfinished business with the McCormack family. He tried the satellite phone to reach Bella.

"Bella." The line crackled, but she knew it was Tuck's voice. "Are you okay?"

"I'm fine. What about you?"

"Good…made it…transponder gone…*Rapid*…" There was so much noise as the signal was fractured, and he sounded like a robot that was falling apart. She could only catch every few words or so.

"What? I can barely hear you. When can I come back

out?"

"...send for you...wait...have to go..." The call cut off. It was only normal. Chances were it was still stormy, and his satellite reception would be spotty.

Still, she was relieved. Tuck was safe. The *Discovery* had survived the storm, which meant all their hard work would still pay off in the cargo they'd already brought up.

S he waited for him to send for her. Days turned into a week. She'd gotten an email from the ship saying they'd lost the transponder signal in the storm, and the floats had been ripped away and found bobbing in the sea. All communication from Tucker was short and to the point. No extended answers. Clearly they were trying to get things put back together and reorient themselves.

The storm had moved the *Rapid*, pulling it down over the rim of the underwater ridge into deep water. To find it, they'd have to start their search all over again, deeper this time. If any of it had survived the drop.

What bothered her worse than the news of losing the *Rapid* were the multiplex containers that kept showing up at Fontanel & Company. She should have been happy having so much that was salvaged from the wreck, and that it all didn't go down again in another hurricane. But each time she opened one she thought of Tuck and wondered why, when he'd been so adamant about being part of her life because of the baby, he wasn't here now.

He still hadn't sent for her. True, they weren't bringing anything new to the surface since they'd lost the wreck, and she had all the work she could handle just processing the artifacts in the multiplex containers. But as weeks became a month, she wondered where they stood. He'd sent an email asking how she and the baby were doing and letting her know he still wanted to talk about their future together, but nothing else. She'd told him the crystal ball was still on the ship and asked to have it sent to her. It never arrived.

At two months of non-stop work and hardly any communication, she was pissed off. Anger slowly replaced the hurt that had lodged itself in her chest. How hard could it be to call, send a damn email, or text message? Was he even still out on the boat? She didn't know. Suspicions began to creep in, prickly, sour thoughts that made her stomach turn. What if he'd decided he didn't want to be a father after all? What if he'd come to a realization out in the storm that life was too short to be burdened by a relationship and a young family?

Even as her heart shrank, her belly began to expand. There was a baby coming, and she refused to let the negativity she was tempted to wallow in impact her child. If she meant anything to Tuck, and she suspected she was fooling herself to think so, he'd be back. Someday. So she waited and went about her life as best as she could.

Chapter Fourteen

William Tucker McCormack peered up at the imposing dark-glass facade of the McCormack Group building in downtown Manhattan. In a few hours, all if it would be his. The thought should have made him happy. It didn't. In fact he was eager to get the deal done and over with and get back to New Orleans to start a life with Bella and the baby.

Since the storm, he'd been pushing himself harder than ever to buy out the McCormack Group and see the defeated look on his half brother's face when he told him he was going to dismantle MCG and sell it off piece by piece. There wasn't a damned thing Tucker wanted that had anything to do with his father, or brother. Getting rid of the company was the last thing he needed to feel like he could separate himself from the family who never wanted to acknowledge his existence, to claim his future as a man free of his past.

As far as Phillip and the board of the McCormack Group knew, it was another company buying them out. Tuck had used a shell company and adroitly kept his name out of the paperwork, letting his lawyers handle everything until he was ready to reveal himself. He wanted to see Phillip's face as the asshole realized who was taking everything from him. He wanted to see his reaction when he realized far from getting rid of the bastard son, their mistreatment of him and his mother had only made him stronger.

He took a deep breath of the city air, laced with the fumes of taxi exhaust, sea brine, and hot dogs being sold on the corner and promised himself a long vacation on his sailing ship with Bella and his child. Five minutes later, he walked past the dark double doors of the boardroom of the McCormack Group. A wall of windows looked over an impressive view of Wall Street and the Hudson, but his attention zeroed in on the lone figure silhouetted against the light streaming in.

Phillip looked no different, only older, than Tuck remembered. More like their father. The slight touch of silver at his temples, the deep blue eyes, and hard features that told the world he bowed to no one. His gut tightened, memories trying to writhe their way up, but he stomped them down, focusing himself on his prey.

"Who let you in here?"

"My attorney."

"Your attor—who are you?"

Tuck angled his head slightly and pulled at the cuff of his Brioni shirt. "Hello, big brother."

The color drained from Phillip's face, leaving him looking pasty and sweating, his shoulders sagged slightly. "It can't be."

"Oh, it most certainly can. And FYI, I met—and exceeded—the provisions of the trust fund several years ago. And as frosting on the cake, I just bought out the McCormack Group lock, stock, and barrel."

Phillip spread his feet aggressively, balancing his fingertips on the polished surface of the boardroom table. He gave Tuck a direct, cold look and asked, his tone mocking. "What are you going to do with a company of this size?"

Tuck leaned forward, flattening his palms on top of the polished table and leaned in for the kill. "Oh, I don't want it. I'm going to dismantle it and sell it off piece by piece."

Phillip frowned. "But why? You'll lose your ass *and* your money."

Tucker smiled mirthlessly. "Because, dickhead, it was never *about* the money."

"But you'll destroy MCG," he said. "The stocks will be worthless." Reality dawned on him, and he blanched further. "You'll ruin us."

"Oh, you mean ruin *your* side of the family? Different when the shoe's on the other foot, isn't it? You didn't give a shit what your actions did to a grieving woman with a child to support, did you? You didn't think what it was like to wonder where your next meal was coming from, or how long you'd be able to afford heat in winter, or if you'd even have a place to sleep that night. Somehow I think you'll find a way to get by, even if you all have to go get *actual* jobs. At least Belladonna Dupré seemed to think you could manage."

The nauseated look on Phillip's face faded a bit as color returned swiftly to his cheeks, and his dark blue eyes grew sharp. "Bella? How the hell do you know Bella?"

Tuck's grin got even bigger. He was sure he was showing all his teeth in a shark's smile. "She's going to be my wife."

Phillip sank into the chair at the head of the long table. Sitting back, he picked the Mont Blanc pen up from the table next to the stack of papers he'd signed and twirled the pen around his fingers. "Please don't tell me you went to all the effort to look her up and screw her just to get back at me. That would be the height of pathetic."

Phillip's feeble attempt to goad him showed how desperate his brother was…and how much Tuck had grown. He didn't need his father or his family's approval. He was his own man, and Phillip's jabs no longer hit home. "As a matter of fact, we met by accident working on the same job. She almost refused to work with me because I reminded her too much of you."

"Heartbroken?"

"Nauseated. Whatever you did to her made her loathe you."

Phillip shrugged, as if Bella meant nothing. Tuck bristled, his hands closing into fists. "Bella was a little too bookish for my taste, and obsessive. She ever find that little boat of hers that she never stopped talking about?"

"Yes."

"And did she find her sunken treasure?" he said, a mocking tone in his voice as he made quotation marks with his fingers around the words sunken treasure.

Tuck brushed off the instant urge to punch him in the face and instead chose to turn it back on him. "I helped her do so."

Phillip's expression changed, his brows knitting together and he stood up, the sharp, poisonous look still in his eyes. "So you left her to come here to take me on?"

"And when I get back we have a wedding and a baby shower to plan." At this point not strictly true, but it would be as soon as he went back to New Orleans. The words came out, intended to wound Phillip, but the minute he'd said it aloud Tuck realized he meant them. He'd resisted the idea of marriage for so long, and love for even longer, that he hadn't even seen the desire for both of them creep up on him.

"Bella is *pregnant*?"

"She is. We're both thrilled." Again a supposition he'd turn into reality as soon as he was able. She had a shitload of things to forgive him for, her pregnancy was one them. He'd fix things with her. He loved her more than he thought he'd ever loved anyone. Pregnant or not, he wanted to marry her. He'd figure things out. Make them work. He had to.

"Don't worry, you won't be expected to clear time in your

schedule for either one. You're not invited." His composure slipped a little. What if, after all this time away setting up the necessary paperwork and money to orchestrate this takeover, Bella wanted nothing to do with him? She was stubborn and opinionated and had a streak of pride a mile wide. Could she, hell *would* she, forgive him? God, he hoped so.

"You're still an idiot, you know that?"

Tuck tried to shove the worries about Bella aside. This was his moment to throw things down with Phillip, and he couldn't let it slip by. "Bitter much? It's a good look for you. Now your outsides match your insides, dickhead."

Phillip put his hands on his hips, spoiling the line of the black Brooks Brothers jacket. "You still don't get it do you?" His handsome face, so similar to their father's, twisted with distaste. "You had it all. The girl. A life of freedom to do whatever the hell you wanted with it. All without being encumbered by all of this." He jerked his chin to indicate the corporate boardroom walls around them. "And you blew it" — he snapped his fingers and gave a mirthless laugh—"just like that. You left her when she was probably her most vulnerable to come here and orchestrate a takeover. That had to take some time, a month at least, maybe more. Women like Bella don't forget shit like that. And from experience, I can tell you she's not the type to forgive or forget. You might have won the battle, William, but you lost the war."

Tuck's gut took a dive to the vicinity of his polished shoes. Yeah, he'd screwed up. Big time. He knew that. *Now.*

He'd let his drive to fix his past overshadow his future and potentially lost out on something far more valuable—a family of his own. A wife. A child. A home he could come back to no matter how far the adventures in his life took him.

The triumphant gleam in Phillip's eye only rubbed salt in the wound, making the sting that much sharper. He'd crafted one of the most brilliant hostile takeovers in decades and gotten credit for finding the *Rapid*. And it made no difference at all. He wasn't getting the satisfaction he'd imagined, and by being so damned one track about this takeover, he'd ignored his own instincts. He should've listened to the little nagging doubts he'd shoved aside. He should never have left Bella alone. All he really wanted was to go back home to New Orleans.

Home...the thought struck him. He'd never had a place he really thought of as home until now. And it wasn't a place, it was a person—a woman with green eyes like the sea on a summer's day, whose bright smile and sassy mouth could make all the pain, all the angst, fade away with just a kiss of her soft lips.

He glanced at the corporate boardroom, the epicenter of power for the McCormack family, cold and pristine...and realized he didn't want it, not one bit of it. Tuck picked up the papers Phillip had just signed, the papers that gave him control of every aspect of the McCormack Group, and tore them in half. The sheets fluttered down to the smooth slate gray carpeting.

Phillip narrowed his eyes. "What's your game, William?"

"It's Tucker, and this is no game."

Phillip sneered at him, crossing his arms. "You really have lost your mind."

Tuck smiled. "No, I think, I've actually found it. You can keep the company, Phillip. I don't need it. And I don't need you or anyone else in the family. In fact, I might even change my name."

Phillip's brow furrowed with confusion, but Tuck didn't stay to find out why. He didn't care. All he wanted to do was get on the next flight back to New Orleans so he could begin to make things right with Bella.

It was dusk and the shadows collected in the corners and crevices of her family home. Bella never knew how tired she could be until she'd hit the first trimester of her pregnancy. What was it about babies that had the ability to siphon off both your energy and your brain? She brushed her teeth to get ready for bed. It didn't matter that she'd skipped dinner; her stomach was too touchy to want to eat. Right now she needed sleep more than food.

She was drifting off when there was a knock at the front door. Min was still at work at the shop so there was no one but her to hear the echo of the heavy iron knocker as it reverberated on the marble in the entryway. When she had a home of her own, she'd have wood floors and soft rugs. She sighed, flipped off her blankets, and padded down the stairs.

The marble tiles were cool against her bare feet. She opened the door a crack and peered out to see Tucker standing there in a business suit, shirt, and a blue power tie worthy of Wall Street. Bella's fingers tightened around the door as her uneven heartbeat increased and her breathing became ragged. "Tucker?"

"Forgotten me already?" His mouth tipped up in a halfhearted smile. A fragile smile.

For a second Bella was too stunned to breathe. He looked so good. So different from the man, the lover, she'd known on the *Discovery*. Perhaps this was the real him, the McCormack him. Dressed in his powerbroker suit, she didn't know him at all. "What are you doing here?"

He frowned. "I came back for you like I said I would."

"Yes, two damned *months* ago. What the hell do you want?"

Tuck glanced up and down the street. "Can I come in? Might be easier if we talked inside."

She rubbed her forehead with shaking fingers, trying to ease the ache that was building behind her eyes. "Yeah, of course, come in." She closed the door, slid off the chain latch, and opened it wide so he could enter. Turning, she left him to close it and walked ahead to the living room. Curling up on the old, familiar couch, she tucked her feet beneath her. Lord, she was crazy happy to see him, but she wasn't going to make this easy on him. He had a lot of explaining to do, and she'd give him enough rope to hang himself before she asked him politely to leave. He had no right to disappear for months on end without a word. He had no right to make her believe he loved her.

Bella gave him a cool look as he took a nearby chair. "Well?"

God, she was beautiful.

How in such a short time had he forgotten the silky texture of her hair, how it gleamed in the low light of evening, or how dark the lashes were that framed those pale green eyes? There were subtle changes, things he didn't think were memory lapse. Her frame looked slightly thinner, but her breasts were larger. He avoided the temptation of touching her.

"How are you?"

"How *am* I?" She gave him an incredulous look. "I'm three months pregnant, morning sick, afternoon sick, and just for fun, evening sick, too. My ankles are swollen, and all I want to eat are pickles. My lover disappeared for months on end without so much as a damn word, and Aunt Min is worried sick about me. *That's* how the hell I am, Tucker. Not that you have a right to know any of that."

"It's good to see you." He faltered. There was an awkwardness between them that had never been there before. Tuck chalked it up to her being hurt and him feeling like a dick for hurting her. He'd told her on the satellite call from the ship he'd be going to New York. He'd gotten caught up in the whirlwind of making the takeover happen and getting the artifacts back to her and had no personal time at all.

"I'm sorry, Bella, I know it took longer than I intended, but—"

"How long did you *intend* to abandon me? No more than a month? Six weeks? Until our baby turned eighteen? I want to know what the hell your plan was. I want to know—" Her voice broke. "How could you leave me alone, wondering what the hell happened to you?"

"I'm sorry."

When the cold look in her eyes refused to thaw, and she didn't respond, he realized he was in way deeper shit than he'd anticipated. He tried again. "I was taking care of some personal business so I could come back to you."

"Were you? Well, it would have been fucking nice if you'd let me know!" she yelled, chucking a pillow from the couch at him. "Did you forget how to pick up a phone? Did you lose the use of both your thumbs and become unable to text? Tell me, Tuck, if I was so important to you—if our child was so important to you—then why didn't you come sooner? Why the hell did you leave me alone?"

She sobbed, and it tore a hole in his heart. He'd been so focused on getting rid of his past, he'd forgotten to embrace his future and now it was slipping like sand through his fingers. He wanted to tell her about his plans for the future—their future. But a bullet of doubt was lodged in his chest making it hard to breathe, and his chest ached with each beat of his heart. What if she wouldn't forgive him?

"I'm sorry. I was an idiot. I was trying to get rid of my demons so I could be a decent father. I just had to—"

"We all have crap in our past, but you can't do this. You can't leave me alone wondering what happened to you and think this is all right."

"You're right. You're 100 percent, totally right."

"And where's the crystal ball? You never answered me, never sent it."

Panic tore through his system, sending shockwaves of alternating cold and heat through him. "I sold it."

Her head shot up. "You *what*?"

"I needed to finance the takeover of the McCormack Group in a hurry, and it was the only piece that could help me get my hands on that much cash. So I sold it."

Bella uncurled her legs and put her feet flat on the floor. Her face was pink, and her fingers curled into fists. And while the rest of her looked like steam was about to come out of her ears, her pale green eyes were like chips of ice—cold, unforgiving. She stood up in one fluid movement and strode over to him and slapped him hard.

"That was mine. Mine! Not yours. *My* family's history. *My* family's curse. Did you think because you slept with me it gave you carte blanche to fuck up my finances as well? What gave you a right to steal from me? What damn right did you have to sell my property? God, I thought you leaving me would kill me. But this— *This* is beyond too much, Tucker. I deserve better than this."

"I did it so I could come back to you a changed man, a man ready to settle down, to do right by his family." Ashamed, embarrassed, filled with emotions too complicated to name, he kept his eyes on her. "No, I didn't. Bella, this is no excuse, but I've spent most of my life plotting to ruin my sperm donor and his legitimate son. The obsession blinded me to the exclusion of all else. The crystal ball became a means to an end. *My* end."

"And not once did you think to *ask* me what *I* wanted. *Your* wants and needs superseded mine. Is *that* how you express your love, Tuck? You say this was revenge for the way your father and his legitimate family treated you and your mother. Fine, you should've figured out how to do that without stealing *someone else's dream*. I've spent my entire life attempting to find the *Rapid* and that crystal ball. The crystal ball was supposed to change *my* life, my *family's* life, for the better. You financed the salvage and *stole* from me. That sure as hell doesn't say, Bella, I love you. It says, Bella, I don't give a damn about you *or* your happiness."

"That's not true. I did it for— Okay. Shit. No. You're right. I was selfish as hell. You're right about all of it." Tuck plowed his fingers through his slicked-back hair, ruining his polished look. "I'll get it back for you. I didn't buyout the company after all. I realized there were more important things to me than getting back at the McCormacks for screwing up my life."

She crossed her arms. "From this side, it looks like you've done a fantastic job screwing up things all on your own. You didn't need them."

"You're right. I was a moron, and I had no damn right to take something you valued as much as that crystal ball. But I was desperate, Bella. Desperate and scared that I wasn't enough for you. I thought that by buying out my half brother I could make things right. I'd own a multimillion-dollar corporation, and I could come back to you—*un*screwed up, without all that emotional baggage I've been carrying around for years. But I realized, almost too late, that it isn't a corporation I need, it wasn't validating what the McCormacks put my mother through and paying them back. When I confronted my half brother with the buyout, I realized I'd been chasing revenge for so long, I didn't need or want it anymore. I don't need *them*, but I do need *you*. I love you, Belladonna Dupré."

He bent down on one knee before her, pulling the box from his pocket that he'd been carrying since his second day in New York. It was his reminder of what he intended to do, of what mattered.

"Bella, I'm an idiot when it comes to doing the right thing in relationships and family, but I hope, I pray, you'll still consider being my wife."

"Get up. You don't have to do this because of the baby."

"What makes you think it's because of the baby?"

"Because you're loyal to a fault. Generous to those you care about, and you'd tear yourself inside out to do the right thing. I've seen it every day since I've met you. You're a good man, misguided but decent, no matter who your family is."

"Does that mean you'll marry me?" He stood up, unable to stop smiling.

"No."

The world came to a dead stop. Tucker was sure the earth wobbled on its axis because the ground shifted out from under him, making him unsteady, even on bended knee before her. All he could hear was the roar of his own pulse in his ears. "But, Bella, I love you."

Her bottom lip trembled a bit. "I don't think you understand what love is. If there's one thing I've learned from the women in my family, it's that love is sacrifice. It's about doing something for someone else at the expense of yourself because you know how much it means to the other person. I believe that you think you're in love with me. But I don't believe you love me. I don't think you know how. If you really loved me, you'd show me I'm the most important thing to you in your actions, not your words." The sadness and heartbreak in her eyes ate through him like acid, leaving a jagged, burning sensation right through the core of him.

"But what about the baby?"

"We Dupré women know how to take care of our own. I'll be fine and so will the baby." She turned away, refusing to look at him. "I think you'd better go."

Tuck staggered to his feet. His world turned dark around

the edges as shock took over, and he went on autopilot. Somehow he made it back to his car. He wasn't even sure how he'd gotten there. He sat there behind the wheel staring straight ahead. Maybe Phillip was right. Maybe he'd screwed up everything in his quest to release his own demons. Maybe Bella was right, and he didn't even know how to love.

He'd avoided it for so long, how could he even start to understand it?

Her words tumbled back over him in a rush, each one a pointed barb that dug in deep and tore him apart.

Sacrifice. Bella had said love meant sacrifice. He'd offered her marriage. What more of a sacrifice could a man like him who'd avoided it like the plague all his life make? Tuck slammed his hand against the steering wheel in frustration and cursed.

Fuck it. He needed a drink.

Later that night, after far too many drinks had made his anxiety and loathing fuzzy around the edges, Tuck sat on a park bench at the edge of Jackson Square, staring at the steps that led to the visitors' center. Even at this late hour, tourists walked in and out of Café Du Monde for a taste of the city. The warm, humid air buzzed with the sounds of cicadas in the trees and a faint, muddy breeze stirred off the river. Where had he gone wrong?

The crystal ball. Maybe the damn thing *was* cursed.

Tuck forced his fuzzy brain to think back. Bella had been angry he'd been so bad at communicating with her while he'd been working on the business deal of the century, but she'd been more pissed about him selling the crystal ball. It meant more than quick cash to her. He knew that. He shouldn't have underestimated its inherent value to her.

What could he do to show her the truth? That he loved her, hell, needed her?

Sacrifice.

That's what she said love meant. She didn't want his money. But she had debts. He knew that when he'd done his fiscal research on the recovery project before he'd ever approached Mr. Palmer. Without buying out the McCormack Group, he had more than enough to pay off her debts. He'd do that first, but deep down he knew that wouldn't be enough.

Bella loved this city. She loved her family. She loved history and had worked so hard to make the recovery of the *Rapid* a possibility. He took another shot of bourbon and let it trail hotly down his throat. Bella was worth fighting for. He needed a gesture. A *big* gesture. Something that would let her know he cared about what mattered to her. *Her* dreams. He tossed what was left of the bottle into a trashcan. Time to stop drinking and use his skills to formulate a plan. He was about to lay siege to Belladonna Dupré.

Chapter Fifteen

Bella stared out the window of Fontanel & Company at the changing leaves. Traffic ebbed and flowed and a long, black limousine pulled up at the curb outside the building. Now that she was well into her second trimester, it was getting harder to move. She'd had plenty of time to analyze Tuck's reason for doing what he'd done once she'd gotten past the blinding red anger that had washed away all reason. Considering her own single-minded determination to recover the *Rapid* and find the crystal ball, could she fault him for being single-minded about his own personal quest?

Yes, she could. But should she? She was still mad and hurt that he'd taken that decision out of her hands. That hadn't been his call to make. But being angry at him, being unforgiving, was punishing her as much as it must be punishing him. She missed him every moment of every day. She loved him, but they couldn't resolve anything between them if he insisted on disappearing just because she told him to go.

She'd told him to leave…and he had. Didn't he have any clue that pregnant women could be emotionally unpredictable? Yes, of course she'd been mad, but when she told him to leave, she'd meant for the night. Maybe for a day or two. Definitely not for forever. But the curse didn't care.

And while her scientific mind still couldn't accept the fact that such a thing existed as a curse, her heart knew better. The Dupré curse had gotten to her just as surely as it had her mother and her aunt, her grandmother and her great-grandmother. Would it ruin her daughter's life as well? The baby kicked, and Bella splayed her hand over her belly. "Don't you worry. Mama will find a way to make sure the curse never touches you." The ultrasound last week had revealed her daughter's developing form, and while she was thrilled to see her baby, she was also sad Tuck wasn't there to share it with her. The simple fact was she missed him. She was still mad as hell at him, but she missed him.

Her office phone rang, and she turned away from the window to pick it up.

"Doctor Dupré, you have a visitor."

Bella sighed. She assumed it was one of the avid collectors who were snatching up items from the *Rapid* as fast as Fontanel & Company could put them up for bid. "Have them come up."

"Actually, they'd prefer if you came down."

Bella pressed the tips of her fingers against the dull ache starting between her eyes. "Fine, I'll be down in a few minutes." *After a quick trip to the bathroom*, she added silently. She hung up and walked out of her office.

Down in the lobby of Fontanel & Company a chauffeur in a black suit and cap and crisp white shirt waited for her. He tipped his cap as she approached. "Doctor Dupré?"

"Yes, I'm Doctor Dupré. I understand you wanted to see

me?"

He gave her a smile. "My employer would like to see you, miss."

Bella glanced around the lobby and on either side of the man, her eyes finally drawn to the limo parked at the curb. She lifted one brow. "Is your boss out in the limo?"

The chauffeur extended his hand, indicating the long black car. "Please, this way Doctor Dupré."

Bella huffed. She was not in the mood to be ordered about when her baby was demanding lunch be served. "Is this going to take long?" she asked as she followed him.

"No, miss. We're very close, but too far to walk," he said as he opened the car door for her and held her hand to help her inside the limo.

The seats were buttery soft black leather, and she sat back as they pulled away from the curb. "So who exactly is your employer?" she asked from the rear seat. She figured it wasn't a kidnapping. Who'd want a broke, pregnant woman who was pining for a man who was too pigheaded to talk things through?

"A great admirer of your work. My employer has been particularly impressed with your recent discovery of the *Rapid* and has been purchasing a number of the items you've auctioned off."

A collector. Bella shifted in her seat. Making nice with the well-financed people who bought art and antiquities was both a skill and a necessity in her line of work. Fine. She'd make nice with the collector. Perhaps go to lunch and earn another commission for her sale.

A few minutes later the limo pulled up just outside the Café Du Monde across from Jackson Park. Surely if he had enough money to purchase the artifacts she'd been selling, he could have picked somewhere more expensive for lunch. "Are we meeting him here?" she asked as the driver opened her door.

"No, miss. Across the street."

Bella glanced at the beautiful old building that had been recently restored. She'd noticed the new paint and the rehabilitation of the ornate stonework in the last two months. Someone had sunk a pretty penny into refurbishing it. The driver escorted her across the street and opened the large double brass and glass doors for her.

A woman dressed in a crisp blue business suit and heels waited for her. "Doctor Dupré?"

"Yes."

"Good afternoon, I'm Aubrey Wilmont, the curator. Would you please follow me?"

A new museum? A new art gallery? There was no signage on the door or outside the building to indicate exactly what kind of business was housed in this wonderful old building. Whatever it was, it would have something to do with the treasure acquired from the *Rapid*. That was good news and could be incredibly lucrative.

The restoration of the building was exquisite and spoke to her love of art and history. She wanted to spend more time enjoying it, but the woman's heels tip-tapped on the cream marble floors so quickly it was hard enough moving her cumbersome body to keep up. Curiosity was eating away at Bella as they walked into the large marble entryway with a bubbling fountain, and huge signs advertised the find of the century and sailing ships from the era of the *Rapid*.

"Excuse me, Ms. Wilmont, is this a museum?" There hadn't been any mention of such a thing in the local media. She wondered why anyone would keep something as grand as this, with such a potential to impact the tourism of the city, so hush-hush.

She turned and smiled. "It is, but we haven't had our grand opening yet. That will be next month."

Bella's steps slowed as she passed some of the lit-glass cases. Items she knew by heart were displayed on polished wood pedestals. Items she'd cleaned with her own hands. "Those bottles and dishes are from the *Rapid*."

"Yes, Doctor Dupré. We're proud to feature an excellent collection of artifacts from your discovery."

"Is this museum owned by a private collector?" Perhaps she'd finally get to meet the anonymous collector that had been the chief buyer of the *Rapid*'s artifacts. It made sense now that someone would want to keep the discovery as a cohesive collection.

"I'm afraid that would be me." The familiar male voice sent shivers down Bella's spine. She looked up the marble staircase to see Tucker, dressed in a business suit, descending toward her. For a moment her heart stopped. He looked good; hell, he looked amazing. But inside she fractured a bit. He looked so different from the man she'd fallen in love with out on the open ocean. The easygoing guy who had callused hands and sun-burnished skin.

"That will be all, Miss Wilmont."

She nodded and walked off, leaving Bella frantically thinking of what to do. She grasped the mermaid pendant on her necklace and pulled it back and forth along the chain.

"Hello, Bella."

"I'm surprised to see you. Why did you come back?"

He chuckled. "Always blunt. No filter. That's part of what I love about you. I can always count on you to be honest with me."

She frowned a little. "I wish I could say the same."

"How have you been?" His eyes trailed down to her now-rounded belly. "How is the baby?"

"We're doing fine."

He nodded and held out a hand to her. "I've got something I want to show you."

For a moment Bella hesitated, then slipped her hand into his. The familiar arc of awareness sparked between them, both comforting and exciting at the same time, causing her stomach to swoop and her heartbeat to speed up. The familiar scent of ocean and sea still surrounded him, and God help her, she drank it in with every breath to stave off the ache of longing. He walked with her in silence along the display spaces, the pieces highlighted and shown to their best advantage. He didn't push her to talk, simply walked with her.

In some ways, the silence was comforting. It gave her time to think. Being without him had been much harder than she wanted to admit. And now being this close, his skin against hers, was almost an overload to her senses.

She tried to focus on her surroundings, instead of the man walking beside her and the way her body instinctively sought to be close to his. "I don't understand. What do you have to do with a museum? Did you contract to sell them the *Rapid* artifacts?" She looked around at the elegant, well-lit space with longing then glanced back at Tucker with a small frown. "What is all of this?"

"It's yours."

Bella's steps faltered, and he grasped her hand more tightly. "Careful. I don't want you to fall."

"What do you mean, it's mine?" She searched his face, those familiar blue eyes, that stubborn, chiseled chin, for a sign this was all a joke.

He smiled and led her up a set of marble steps to the gallery beyond. "This museum, The Dupré Museum of Antiquities and Sea History, is yours."

Her frown deepened. "The Dupré Museum of— Why?"

"Because we needed a suitable space to showcase this."

They reached the top of the stairs, and there, in the center of the gallery, spotlighted so it glittered, was the crystal ball from the wreck.

Bella gasped, dropping his hand. "Is that—"

"The crystal ball? Yes. I bought it back, but it didn't seem fitting for it to just sit and gather dust on your aunt's mantle. Not when it could bring so many here to the city and be the centerpiece to show the world what an amazing find you made. You deserve to have the whole world know your name."

She clasped her hands in front of her and brought them to her mouth, like a prayer, her eyes glistening with unshed tears. He was hoping to God he didn't make her cry. "You did this for me?"

He smiled. "Of course I did this for you. There's nothing I wouldn't sacrifice for you."

She turned, tears streaming down her face and grabbed him around the middle, burying her face in his shirt. For a moment he stood, frightened to do anything that might make her cry more. But he couldn't stop himself from touching her, not when she was so close. He wrapped his arms around her, holding her and letting her cry.

The soft scent of lemon and sugar cookies drifted up from her hair, making his heart do a double-clutch with need. God, how he'd missed her. He stroked the silk of her hair and rested his cheek against the top of her head. "Bella, are you okay?"

She nodded, and he let out a sigh of relief. Thank God. If he'd done something else to break her heart, he had no clue how to make up for it. He'd given it everything he had to get the museum renovated and open for business in this short amount of time to show her how much she meant to him.

"It's beautiful," she said softly.

He lifted her chin with the crook of his finger, forcing her to look up into his face. "The diamond?"

She shook her head. "All of it. The museum, the crystal ball, all of it. It's amazing. I never could have pulled off something like this."

"I did it for you."

She smiled. "I know."

"I want the world to know how proud I am of you. How much you've accomplished and to have a place to show all the wonderful things that you've found. There are also teaching labs at the back of the museum so you can give classes if you want."

Her eyes sparkled far more than any diamond could have. "Really?"

"This time I tried to think of everything." He sank down to one knee in front of her and pulled a ring box from his pocket, flipping it open to reveal a three-carat diamond ring. "At the risk of being rejected again, Belladonna Dupré, I love you. I know I've screwed up before, but I want to be with you." He placed a kiss on her belly. "I want to be a father and grow old with you. Will you marry me?"

She nodded. Relief flooded his system. He stood and wrapped his arms around her, pulling her into his chest.

"Yes, I'll marry you. I'll be your wife, the mother of our child—"

"Children," he corrected, leaning his forehead against hers. "I don't know about you, but being an only child sucked most of the time. I'd rather not repeat that for my own kids."

She laughed. "I've always wanted a full house. See, we have way more in common than you ever realized. But there's one thing." She pulled back, looking him in the eye. "I'm not so sure I can become a McCormack."

He gave her a ten-thousand watt grin, plucked the ring from the box, and slid it on her finger. "Good, because I was hoping you'd let me change my name to Dupré."

"What?"

"Never wanted to be a McCormack; still don't see the need. Besides, don't you think Tucker Dupré sounds more southern?"

"Definitely."

"Well, if we're going to raise our children here, they'll need to feel at home."

She glanced at the ring on her finger then looked up at him with a smile that lit up her whole face and melted his heart. "You've always had a home, right here in my heart."

He pulled her close and kissed her. She melted into him, and he realized for the first time in forever he was content, happy to be in this time and place with this woman in his arms. He caressed her face, loving the look that was in her eyes, the one that told him *welcome home, you are loved.* "Do you think fate brought us together?" he asked.

"No," she said and kissed him lightly, the familiar spark arcing between them once again, "but perhaps it was written in the stars."

Acknowledgments

This book would not have been possible without the dedicated team of my editor Alethea Spirndon, my agent Holly Root, my super amazing critique partner Cherry Adair, and the non-writer friends who always have my back, Karla Baehr, Larie Brown and Vivian Jensen. Thank you is not enough. You ladies inspire me, get me back to the keyboard, and keep me smiling with a good cup of tea.

About the Author

A former journalist and public relations officer, author Theresa Meyers couldn't read until after the third grade. Despite her dyslexia, her first national piece was published in *Merlin's Pen* magazine at age 17. She's spent over a quarter of a century married to her Prom date, lives on a mini-farm near Seattle with her family, drinks tea – never coffee, and has been a PADI certified open water diver since the age of 19. When she's not writing she's likely sewing, baking, helping with homework, or riding her horse. Want to know more? Go to www.theresameyers.com

Discover the **Men of the Zodiac** *series…*

IMPULSE CONTROL
Sign: Ares

THE MILLIONAIRE'S DECEPTION
Sign: Taurus

THE MILLIONAIRE'S FOREVER
Sign: Gemini

TEN DAYS IN TUSCANY
Sign: Cancer

THE MILLIONAIRE DADDY PROJECT
Sign: Leo

REVENGE BEST SERVED HOT
Sign: Virgo

THE PRINCE'S RUNAWAY LOVER
Sign: Libra

THE COLONEL'S DAUGHTER
Sign: Scorpio

ONE NIGHT WITH THE BILLIONAIRE
Sign: Sagittarius

THE GREEK TYCOON'S TARNISHED BRIDE
Sign: Capricorn

BLURRING THE LINES
Sign: Aquarius

Also by Theresa Meyers

THE GEEK BILLIONAIRE MAKEOVER

THE SWITCHED BABY SCANDAL

SHADOWLANDER